COLD FEET

Compiled by Jean Richardson
Stories to chill you!

I turned to look back, and saw that the big old farmhouse building was gone, and that all that was left was the low shape of a cottage or hut, no bigger than one of our barns. But there wasn't time to think about that. Water was lapping round my bare feet. I heard a massive creaking, and could just make out the shape of an enormous bulk moving, the hull, masts and all, and riggings, and straining sails, of a galleon.

There was the cry again. This time I knew even before the light came up again what it was. A child was in the water, and he was shouting for help.

Haunting tales to thrill and chill from Robert Westall, Joan Aiken, Antonia Barber, Philip Pullman, Pamela Oldfield, Alison Prince, Jean Richardson and Berlie Doherty.

'Most distinguished.' *The Times Educational Supplement*

**Also by Jean Richardson
and available in Knight Books:**

THE FIRST STEP
DANCER IN THE WINGS
ONE FOOT ON THE GROUND

Cold Feet

Compiled by
Jean Richardson

Hodder and Stoughton

The Boys' Toilets copyright © 1985
Robert Westall
Wing Quack Flap copyright © 1985
Joan Aiken
My Mother's Story copyright © 1985
Antonia Barber
Video Nasty copyright © 1985 Philip
Pullman
Dolling Halt copyright © 1985 Pamela
Oldfield
Nathan's True Self copyright © 1985
Alison Prince
Not at Home copyright © 1985 Jean
Richardson
Ghost Galleon copyright © 1985 Berlie
Doherty

Ghost Galleon was originally
commissioned for a series in a BBC
Radio 4 Schools Programme

This compilation copyright © 1985
Jean Richardson
First published by Hodder & Stoughton
Children's Books 1985
First published by Knight Books 1986
Third impression 1989

British Library C.I.P.

Cold feet
   1. Horror tales, English
   2. Children's stories, English
   I. Richardson, Jean
   823'.01'0816[J]   PZ5

ISBN 0 340 42963 1

Printed and bound in Great Britain
for Hodder and Stoughton
Paperbacks, a division of Hodder and
Stoughton Ltd., Mill Road,
Dunton Green, Sevenoaks, Kent
TN13 2YA.
(Editorial Office: 47 Bedford Square,
London WC1B 3DP) by
Cox & Wyman Ltd., Reading

Contents

The Boys' Toilets *by Robert Westall* 7

Wing Quack Flap *by Joan Aiken* 35

My Mother's Story *by Antonia Barber* 51

Video Nasty *by Philip Pullman* 65

Dolling Halt *by Pamela Oldfield* 75

Nathan's True Self *by Alison Prince* 85

Not at Home *by Jean Richardson* 109

Ghost Galleon *by Berlie Doherty* 119

The Boys' Toilets

by

Robert Westall

The January term started with a scene of sheer disaster.
A muddy excavator was chewing its way across the
netball-court, breakfasting on the tarmac with sinuous
lunges and terrifying swings of its yellow dinosaur neck.
One of the stone balls had been knocked off the gate-
posts, and lay in crushed fragments, like a Malteser
trodden on by a giant. The entrance to the science wing
was blocked with a pile of ochreous clay, and curved
glazed drainpipes were heaped like school dinners'
macaroni.

The girls hung round in groups. One girl came back
from the indoor toilets saying Miss Bowker was phoning
County Hall, and using words that Eliza Bottom had
nearly been expelled for last term. She was greeted with
snorts of disbelief . . .

The next girl came back from the toilet saying Miss
Bowker was nearly crying.

Which was definitely a lie, because here was Miss
Bowker now, come out to address them in her best
sheepskin coat. Though she *was* wearing fresh make-up,
and her eyes were suspiciously bright, her famous chin
was up. She was brief, and to the point. There was
an underground leak in the central heating; till it was
mended, they would be using the old Harvest Road
boys' school. They would march across now, by forms,
in good order, in charge of the prefects. She knew
they would behave immaculately, and that the spirit of
Spilsby Girls' Grammar would overcome all diffi-
culties . . .

'Take more than school spirit,' said Wendy Falstaff.

'More than a bottle of whisky,' said Jennifer Mount, and shuddered. Rebeccah, who was a vicar's daughter, thought of Sodom and Gomorrah; both respectable suburbs by comparison with Harvest Road. Harvest Road was literally on the wrong side of the tracks. But obediently they marched. They passed through the streets where they lived, gay with yellow front doors, picture-windows, new car-ports and wrought-iron gates. It was quite an adventure at first. Staff cars kept passing them, their rear-windows packed with whole classrooms. Miss Rossiter, with her brass microscopes and stuffed ducks; Mademoiselle, full of tape-recorders and posters of the French wine-growing districts. Piles of *The Merchant of Venice* and 'Sunflowers' by Van Gogh . . .

The first time they passed, the teachers hooted cheerfully. But coming back they were silent, just their winkers winking, and frozen faces behind the wheel.

Then the marching columns came to a miserable little hump-backed bridge over a solitary railway-line, empty and rusting. Beyond were the same kind of houses; but afflicted by some dreadful disease, of which the symptoms were a rash of small window-panes, flaking paint, overgrown funereal privet-hedges and sagging gates that would never shut again. And then it seemed to grow colder still, as the slum-clearances started, a great empty plain of broken brick, and the wind hit them full, sandpapering faces and sending grey berets cartwheeling into the wilderness.

And there, in the midst of the desolation, like a dead sooty dinosaur, like a blackened, marooned, many-chimneyed Victorian battleship, lay Harvest Road school.

'Abandon hope all ye who enter here,' said Jennifer Mount.

'We who are about to die salute you,' said Victoria.

Rebeccah thought there were some advantages to having a Classical education after all.

★　　★　　★

They gathered, awed, in the hall. The windows, too high up to see out of, were stained brown round the edges; the walls were dark-green. There was a carved oak board, a list of prize-winners from 1879 till 1923. Victoria peered at it. 'It's B.C., not A.D.,' she announced. 'The first name's Tutankhamun.' There were posters sagging off the walls, on the extreme ends of long hairy strands of sticky tape; things like 'Tea-picking in India' and 'The Meaning of Empire Day'. It all felt rather like drowning in a very dirty goldfish tank.

A lot of them wanted the toilet, badly. Nervousness and the walk through the cold. But nobody felt like asking till Rebeccah did. Last door at the end of the corridor and across the yard; they walked down, six-strong.

They were boys' toilets. They crept past the male mystery of the urinals, tall, white and rust-streaked as tombs, looking absurd, inhuman, like elderly invalid-carriages or artificial limbs. In the bottom gulley, fag-ends lay squashed and dried-out, like dead flies.

And the graffiti . . . even Liza Bottom didn't know what some words meant. But they were huge and hating . . . the whole wall screamed with them, from top to bottom. Most of the hate seemed directed at someone called 'Barney Boko'.

Rebeccah shuddered; that was the first shudder. But Vicky only said practically 'Bet there's no toilet-paper!' and got out her French exercise-book . . . She was always the pessimist; but on this occasion she hadn't been pessimistic enough. Not only no toilet-paper, but no wooden seats either, and the lavatory-chains had been replaced by loops of hairy thick white string, like hangmen's nooses. And in the green paint of the wooden partitions, the hatred of Barney Boko had been gouged half-an-inch deep. And the locks had been bust off all the doors except the far end one . . .

Rebeccah, ever public-spirited and with a lesser need, stood guard stoutly without.

'Boys,' she heard Victoria snort in disgust. 'It's a nunnery for me . . . at least in nunneries they'll have soft toilet-paper.'

'Don't you believe it,' said Joanne, their Roman Catholic correspondent. 'They wear hair-shirts, nuns. Probably the toilets have *scrubbing-brushes* instead of paper.'

Lively squeaks, all down the line, as the implications struck home.

'Some boys aren't bad,' said Liza, 'if you can get them away from their friends.'

'Why bother,' said Vicky. 'I'll settle for my poster of Duran Duran . . .'

'It's funny,' said Tracy, as they were combing their hair in the solitary cracked, fly-spotted, pocket-handkerchief-sized mirror. 'You know there's six of us? Well, I heard *seven* toilets flush. Did anybody pull the chain twice?'

They all looked at each other, and shook their heads. They looked back down the long shadowy loo, with its tiny, high-up pebbled windows, towards the toilets. They shouted, wanting to know who was there, because nobody had passed them, nobody had come in.

No answer, except the sound of dripping.

*   *   *

The big attraction at break was the school boiler-house. They stood round on the immense coke-heaps, some new, some so old and mixed with the fallen leaves of many autumns they were hardly recognisable as coke at all. One actually had weeds growing on it . . .

Inside the boiler-house, in a red hissing glow, two men fought to get Harvest Road up to a reasonable temperature, somewhere above that of Dracula's crypt. One was young, cheerful, cocky, with curly brown hair;

they said he was from County. The other was tall and thin, in a long grey overall-coat and cap so old the pattern had worn off. They said he was the caretaker of the old school, brought out of retirement because only he knew the ropes . . . he had such an expression on his face that they immediately called him Crippen. Occasionally, the cocky one would stop shovelling coke into the gaping red maw of the furnace and wipe his brow; that, and the occasional draught of warm air, immediately swept away by the biting wind, was the only hint of heat they had that morning.

The lesson after break was maths, with Miss Hogg. Miss Hogg was one of the old school; grey hair in a tight bun, tweeds, gold-rimmed spectacles. A brilliant mathematician who had once unbent far enough, at the end of summer term, to tell the joke about the square on the hypotenuse. Feared but not loved, Miss Hogg made it quite clear to all that she had no time for men. Not so much a Female Libber as a Male Oppressor . . .

They ground away steadily at quadratic equations, until the dreary cold, seeping out of the tiled walls into their bones, claimed Rebeccah as its first victim. Her hand shot up.

'You should have gone at break,' said Miss Hogg.

'I did, Miss Hogg.'

Miss Hogg's gesture gave permission, while despairing of all the fatal weaknesses of femininity.

★   ★   ★

Rebeccah hesitated just inside the doorway of the loo. The length of the low dark room, vanishing into shadow; the little green windows high up that lit nothing, the alienness of it all made her hesitant, as in some old dark church. The graffiti plucked at the corners of her eyes, dimly, like memorials on a church wall. But no 'dearly beloveds' here.

JACKO IS A SLIMER

F★★★ OFF HIGGINS.

Where were they now? How many years ago? She told herself they must be grown men, balding, with wives and families and little paunches under cardigans their wives had lovingly knitted for them. But she couldn't believe it. They were still here somewhere, fighting, snorting bubbles of blood from streaming noses, angry. Especially angry with Barney Boko. She went down the long room on tiptoe, and went into the far-end toilet because it was the only one with a lock. Snapped home the bolt so hard it echoed up and down the concrete ceiling. Only then, panting a little, did she settle . . .

But no sooner had she settled than she heard someone come in. Not a girl; Rebeccah had quick ears. No, big boots, with steel heel-plates. Walking authoritatively towards her. From the liveliness of the feet she knew it wasn't even a man. A boy. She heard him pause, as if he sensed her; as if looking round. Then, a boy's voice, quiet.

'O.K., Stebbo, all clear!'

More stamping heel-capped feet tramping in.

She knew she had made a terrible mistake. There must still be a boys' school here; only occupying part of the buildings. And she was in the *boys'* loo. She blushed. An enormous blush that seemed to start behind her ears, and went down her neck over her whole body . . .

But she was a sensible child. She told herself to be calm. Just sit, quiet as a mouse till they'd gone. She sat, breathing softly into her handkerchief, held across her mouth.

But supposing they tried the door, shouted to know who was in there? Suppose they put their hands on the top of the wooden partition and hauled themselves up and looked over the top. There were some awful *girls* who did that . . .

But they seemed to have no interest in her locked cubicle. There was a lot of scuffling, a scraping of steel heel-plates and a panting. As if they were dragging somebody . . .

The somebody was dragged into the cubicle next door. Elbows thumped against the wooden partition, making her jump.

'Get his head down,' ordered a sharp voice.

'No, Stebbo NO! Let me go, you bastards . . .'

'Ouch!'

'What's up?'

'Little sod bit me . . .'

'Get his head down then!'

The sounds of heaving, scraping, panting, and finally a sort of high-pitched whining, got worse. Then suddenly the toilet next door flushed, the whining stopped, then resumed as a series of half-drowned gasps for breath. There was a yip of triumph, laughter, and the noise of many boots running away.

'Bastards,' said a bitter, choking voice. 'And you've broken my pen an' all.' Then a last weary pair of boots trailed away.

She got herself ready, listening, waiting, tensed. Then undid the bolt with a rush and ran down the empty echoing place. Her own footsteps sounded frail and tiny, after the boys. Suppose she met one, coming in?

But she didn't. And there wasn't a boy in sight in the grey high-walled yard. Bolder, she looked back at the entrance of the loo . . . it was the same one they'd used earlier; the one they'd been told to use. Miss Bowker must have made a mistake; someone should be told . . .

But when she got back to the classroom, and Miss Hogg and all the class looked up, she lost her nerve.

'You took your time, Rebeccah,' said Miss Hogg, suspiciously.

'We thought you'd pulled the chain too soon and gone down to the sea-side,' said Liza Bottom, playing for a vulgar laugh and getting it.

'Let me see your work so far, Liza,' said Miss Hogg

frostily, killing the laughter like a partridge shot on the wing.

'What's up?' whispered Vicky. 'You met a fellah or something – all blushing and eyes shining . . .' Vicky was much harder to fool than Miss Hogg.

'Tell you at lunch . . .'

'The next girl I see talking . . .' said Miss Hogg ominously.

But they didn't have to wait till lunch. Liza had twigged that something was up. Her hand shot up; she squirmed in her seat almost too convincingly.

'Very well, Liza. I suppose I must brace myself for an epidemic of weak bladders . . .'

Liza returned like a bomb about to explode, her ginger hair standing out from her head like she'd back-combed it for Saturday night, a deep blush under her freckles and green eyes wide as saucers. She opened her mouth to speak . . . but Miss Hogg had an eagle eye for incipient hysteria, and a gift for nipping it in the bud.

'Shut the door, Liza, we'll keep the draughts we have.' Liza sat down demurely; but even the Hogg's frost couldn't stop the idea flaring across the class that something was excitingly amiss in the loos. It was droopy Margie Trawson who blew it. She went next; and came back and bleated, with that air of a victimised sheep that only she could achieve.

'Miss, there's boys in the toilet . . .'

'Boys?' boomed Miss Hogg. 'BOYS?' She swept out of the classroom door with all the speed her strongly-muscled legs could give her. From the classroom windows, they watched as she entered the toilets. Rebeccah, who was rather keen on naval warfare in World War II, thought she looked like an angry little frigate, just itching to depth-charge any boy out of existence. But when she emerged, her frown told that she'd been cheated of her prey. She scouted on for boys lurking behind the coke-heaps, behind the dustbins, behind the sagging fence of the caretaker's house. Nothing. She looked back towards her classroom windows, making every girlish head duck simultaneously, then headed for the Headmistress's office.

In turn, they saw the tall stately figure of the Head inspect the loo, the coke-heaps, fence and dustbins, Miss Hogg circling her on convoy-duty. But without success. Finally, after a word, they parted. Miss Hogg returned, with a face like thunder.

'Someone,' she announced, 'has been silly. Very, *very*, silly.' She made 'silly' sound as evil as running a concentration camp. 'The Head has assured me that this school has been disused for many years, and there cannot possibly be a single boy on the premises. The only . . . males . . . are the caretakers. Now, Margie, what have you got to say to *that*? Well . . . Margie . . . *well*?'

There was only one end to Miss Hogg's well-Margie-well routine. Margie gruesomely dissolving into tears. 'There was boys Miss, I heard them Miss, honeeest . . .' She pushed back a tear with the cuff of her cardigan.

Liza was on her feet, flaming. 'I heard them too, Miss.' That didn't worry Miss Hogg. Liza was the form trouble-maker. But then Rebeccah was on her feet. 'I heard them as well.'

'*Rebeccah* – you are a clergyman's daughter. I'm ashamed of you.'

'I *heard* them.' Rebeccah clenched her teeth; there would be no shifting her. Miss Hogg looked thoughtful.

'They don't come when you're in a crowd, Miss,' bleated Margie. 'They only come when you're there by yourself. They put another boy's head down the toilet an' pulled the chain. They were in the place next to me.'

'And to me,' said Liza.

'And to me,' said Rebeccah.

A sort of shiver went round the class; the humming and buzzing stopped, and it was very quiet.

'Very well,' said Miss Hogg. 'We will test Margie's theory. *Come*, Rebeccah!'

At the entrance to the toilet, Rebeccah suddenly felt very silly.

'Just go in and behave normally,' said Miss Hogg. 'I shall be just outside.'

Rebeccah entered the toilet, bolted the door and sat down.

'Do exactly what you would normally do,' boomed Miss Hogg, suddenly, scarily, down the long dark space. Rebeccah blushed again, and did as she was told.

'There,' boomed Miss Hogg, after a lengthy pause. 'Nothing, you see. Nothing at all. You girls are *ridiculous*!' Rebeccah wasn't so sure. There was something – you couldn't call it a sound – a sort of vibration in the air, like boys giggling in hiding.

'Nothing,' boomed Miss Hogg again. 'Come along – we've wasted enough lesson-time. Such nonsense.'

Suddenly a toilet flushed, at the far end of the row.

'Was that you, Rebeccah?'

'No, Miss Hogg.'

'Rubbish. Of course it was.'

'No, Miss.'

Another toilet flushed; and another; getting nearer. That convinced Miss Hogg. Rebeccah heard her stout brogues come in at a run, heard her banging back the toilet-doors, shouting,

'Come out, whoever you are. You can't get away. I know you're there.'

Rebeccah came out with a rush to meet her.

'Did you pull your chain, Rebeccah?'

'Didn't need to, Miss.'

And indeed, all the toilet doors were now open, and all the toilets manifestly empty, and every cistern busy refilling; except Rebeccah's.

'There must be a scientific explanation,' said Miss Hogg. 'A fault in the plumbing.'

But Rebeccah thought she heard a quiver in her voice, as she stared suspiciously at the small, inaccessible ventilation grids.

*　　*　　*

They all went together at lunchtime; and nothing happened. They all went together at afternoon break, and nothing happened. Then it was time for Miss Hogg again. Black Monday was called Black Monday because they had Miss Hogg twice for Maths.

And still the cold worked upon their systems . . .

Margie Trawson again.

'Please, Miss, I *got* to.'

Only . . . there was a secret in Margie's voice, a little gloaty secret. They all heard it; but if Miss Hogg did, she only raised a grizzled eyebrow. 'Hurry, then . . . if only your *mind* was so active, Margie.'

She was gone a long time; a very long time. Even Miss Hogg shifted her brogued feet restlessly, as she got on with marking the other third-year form's quadratic equations.

And then Margie was standing in the doorway, and behind her, the looming grey-coated figure of Crippen, with his mouth set so hard and cruel, another poisoning was obviously imminent. He had Margie by the elbow, in a grip that made her writhe. He whispered to Miss Hogg . . .

'Appalling,' boomed Miss Hogg. 'I don't know what these children think they are coming to. Thank you for telling me so quickly, caretaker. It won't happen again. I assure you, it won't happen again. That will be all!'

Crippen, robbed of his moment of public triumph and infant-humiliation, stalked out without another word.

'Margie,' announced Miss Hogg, 'has attempted to use the caretaker's outside toilet. The toilet set aside for his own personal use. A *man's* toilet . . .'

'Obviously a hanging offence,' muttered Victoria,

sotto voce, causing a wild but limited explosion of giggles, cut off as by a knife, by Miss Hogg's glint-spectacled *look*. 'How would you like it, Margie, if some strange men came into your backyard at home and used *your* toilet?'

'It'd really turn her on,' muttered Victoria. Liza choked down on a giggle so hard, she nearly gave herself a slipped disc.

'No girl will ever do such a thing again,' said Miss Hogg in her most dreadful voice, clutching Margie's elbow as cruelly as Crippen had. A voice so dreadful and so seldom heard that the whole form froze into thoughtfulness. Not since that joke with the chewing-gum in the first year had they heard *that* voice.

'Now, Margie, will you go and do what you have to do, in the place where you are meant to do it.'

'Don't want to go no more, Miss. It's gone off . . .'

Liar, thought Rebeccah; Margie needed to go so badly, she was squirming from foot to foot.

'GO!' said Miss Hogg, in the voice that brooked no argument. 'I shall watch you from the window.'

They all watched her go in; and they all watched her come out.

'Sit down quickly, Margie,' said Miss Hogg. 'There seems to be some difficulty with question twelve. It's quite simple really.' She turned away to the blackboard, chalk in hand. 'X squared, plus 2y . . .' The chalk squeaked abominably, getting on everyone's nerves; there was a slight but growing disturbance at the back of the class, which Miss Hogg couldn't hear for the squeaking of the chalk . . . '3x plus 5y' . . .

'Oh, *Miss*!' wailed Margie. 'I'm sorry, Miss . . . I didn't mean to . . .' Then she was flying to the classroom door, babbling and sobbing incoherently. She scrabbled for the door-knob and finally got it open. Miss Hogg moved across swiftly and tried to grab her, but she was just too slow; Margie was gone, with Miss Hogg in hot pursuit, hysterical sobs and angry shouts echoing round the whole school from the pair of them.

'What . . .?' asked Rebeccah, turning. Vicky pointed silently, at a wide spreading pool of liquid under Margie's desk.

'She never went at all,' said Vicky grimly. 'She must have hidden just inside the loo doorway. She was too scared . . .'

It was then that Rebeccah began to hate the ghosts in the boys' toilets.

*   *   *

She tapped on Dad's study door, as soon as she got in from school. Pushed it open. He was sitting, a tall thin boyish figure, at his desk with the desk-light on. From his dejectedly drooping shoulders, and his spectacles pushed up on his forehead, she knew he was writing next Sunday's sermon. He was bashing between his eyes with a balled fist as well; Epiphany was never his favourite topic for a sermon.

'Dad?'

He came back from far away, pulled down his spectacles, blinked at her and smiled.

'It's the Person from Porlock!' This was a very ancient joke between them, that only got better with time. The real Person from Porlock had interrupted the famous poet Coleridge, when he was in the middle of composing his greatest poem, 'Kubla Khan'.

'Sit down, Person,' said Dad, removing a precarious tower of books from his second wooden armchair. 'Want a coffee?' She glanced at his percolator; shiny and new from Mum last Christmas, but now varnished-over with dribbles, from constant use.

'Yes please,' she said, just to be matey; he made his coffee as strong as poison.

'How's Porlock?' He gave her a sharp sideways glance through his horn-rimmed spectacles. 'Trouble?'

Somehow, he always knew.

She was glad she could start at the beginning, with ordinary things like the central heating and the march to Harvest Road . . .

When she had finished, he said 'Ghosts. Ghosts in the toilet. Pulling chains and frightening people.' He was the only adult she knew who wouldn't have laughed or made some stupid remark. But all he said was 'Something funny happened at that school. It was closed down. A few years before Mum and I came to live here. It had an evil name; but I never knew for what.'

'But what can we *do*? The girls are terrified.'

'Go at lunchtime – go at break – go before you leave home.'

'We do. But it's so cold – somebody'll get caught out sooner or later.'

'You won't be at Harvest Road long – even central heating leaks don't go on for ever. Shall I try to find out how long? I know the Chairman of Governors.'

'Wouldn't do any harm,' said Rebeccah grudgingly.

'But you don't want to wait to go that long?' It was meant to be a joke; but it died halfway between them.

'Look,' said Rebeccah, 'if you'd seen Margie . . . she . . . she won't dare come back. Somebody could be . . . terrified for life.'

'I'll talk to your Headmistress . . .' He reached for the phone.

'NO!' It came out as nearly a shout. Dad put the phone back, looking puzzled. Rebeccah said, in a low voice,

'The teachers think we're nuts. They'll . . . think you're nuts as well. You . . . can't afford to have people think *you're* nuts. Can you?'

'Touché,' he said ruefully. 'So what do you want, Person?'

'Tell me how to get rid of them. How to frighten them away, so they leave people *alone*.'

'I'm not in the frightening business, Person.'

'But the church . . .'

'You mean . . . bell, book and candle? No can do. The church doesn't like that kind of thing any more . . . doesn't believe in it, I suppose . . .'

'But it's *real*.' It was almost a wail.

'The only man I know who touches that sort of thing has a parish in London. He's considered a crank.'

'*Tell me what to do!*'

They looked at each other in silence, a very long time. They were so much alike, with their blonde hair, long faces, straight noses, spectacles. Even their hair was the same length; he wore his long; she wore hers shortish.

Finally he said, 'There's no other way?'

'No.'

'I don't know much. You're supposed to ask its name. It has to tell you – that's in the Bible. That's supposed to give you power over it. Then, like Shakespeare, you can ask it whether it's a spirit of health or goblin damned. Then . . . you can try commanding it to go to the place prepared for it . . .' He jumped up, running his fingers through his hair. 'No, you mustn't do any of this, Rebeccah. I can't have you doing things like this. I'll ring the Head . . .'

'You will NOT!'

'Leave it alone, then!'

'If it lets me alone.' But she had her fingers crossed.

*   *   *

The Head came in to address them next morning, after assembly. She braced her long elegant legs wide apart, put her hands together behind her back, rocked a little, head down, then looked at them with a smile that was a hundred per cent caring, and about ninety per cent honest.

'Toilets,' she said doubtfully, then with an effort, more briskly, 'Toilets.' She nodded gently. 'I can understand you are upset about the toilets. Of all the things about this dreadful place that County's put us in, those toilets are the worst. I want you to know that I have had the strongest possible words with County, and that those toilets will be repainted and repaired by next Monday morning. I have told them that if they fail me in this, I will close the school.' She lowered her head in deep thought again, then looked up, more sympathetic than ever.

'You have reached an age when you are – quite rightly – beginning to be interested in boys. There *have* been boys here – they have left their mark – and I am sad they have left the worst possible kind of mark. Most boys are not like that – not like that at all, thank God. But – these boys have been *gone* for over twenty years. Let me stress that. For twenty years, this building has been used to store unwanted school furniture. You may say that there are always boys everywhere – like mice, or beetles! But with all this slum-clearance around us . . . I went out yesterday actually *looking* for a boy.' She looked round with a smile, expecting a laugh. She got a few titters. 'The first boy I saw was a full mile away – and he was working for a butcher in the High Street.' Again, she expected a laugh, and it did not come. So she went serious again. 'You have been upset by the toilets – understandably. But that is no excuse for making things up – for, and I must say it, getting hysterical. Nobody else has noticed anything in these toilets. The prefects report nothing – I have watched first and second years using them quite happily. *It is just this class.* Or rather, three excitable girls in this class . . .' She looked round. At Liza Bottom, who blushed and wriggled. At the empty desk where Margie should have been sitting. And at Rebeccah, who stared straight back at her, as firmly as she could. 'Two of those girls do not surprise me – the third girl does.' Rebeccah did not flinch, which worried the Head, who was rather fond of her. So the Head finished in rather a rush. 'I want you to stop acting as feather-brained females – and act instead as the sensible, hard-headed young women you are going to become. This business . . . is the sort of business that gets us despised by men . . . and there are plenty of men only too ready to despise us.'

The Head swept out. A sort of deadly coldness settled over the sensible young women. It hadn't happened to the prefects, or to the first years. The Head had just proved there were ghosts, and proved they were only after people in 3A . . .

*   *   *

It was Fiona Mowbray who bought it. It happened so swiftly, after break. They'd all gone together at break. They never realised they'd left her there, helpless with diarrhoea, and too shy to call out. She was always the shyest, Fiona . . .

Suddenly she appeared in the doorway, interrupting the beginning of French.

'Sit down, Feeownah,' said Mamselle, gently.

But Fiona just stood there, pale and stiff as a scarecrow, swaying. There were strange twists of toilet-paper all round her arms . . .

'Feeownah,' said Mamselle again with a strange panicky quiver in her voice. Fiona opened and closed her mouth to speak four times, without a single sound coming out. Then she fainted full-length, hitting the floorboards like a sack of potatoes.

Then someone ran for the Head, and everyone was crowding round, and the Head was calling stand back give her air and sending Liza for Miss Hogg's smelling salts. And Fiona coming round and starting to scream and flail out. And fainting again. And talk of sending for a doctor . . .

Right, you sod, thought Rebeccah. That's *it*! And she slipped round the back of the clustering crowd, and nobody saw her go, for all eyes were on Fiona.

Fiona must have been in the third toilet . . . the toilet-roll holder was empty, and the yellow paper, swathe on swathe of it, covered the floor and almost buried the lavatory-bowl. It was wildly torn in places, as if Fiona had had to claw her way out of it. Had it . . . been trying to smother her? Rebeccah pulled the chain automatically. Then, with a wildly-beating heart, locked herself in the next door, and sat down with her jaw clenched and her knickers round her knees.

It was hard to stay calm. The noise of the re-filling cistern next door hid all other noises. Then, as next-door dropped to a trickle, she heard another toilet being pulled. Had someone else come in, unheard? Was she wasting her time? But there'd been no footsteps. Then another toilet flushed, and another and another. Then the doors of the empty toilets began banging, over and over, so hard and savagely that she thought they must splinter.

Boom, boom, boom. Nearer and nearer.

Come on, bastard, thought Rebeccah, with the hard centre of her mind; the rest of her felt like screaming.

Then the toilet pulled over her own head. So violently it showered her with water. She looked up, and the hairy string was swinging, with no one holding it . . . like a hangman's noose. Nobody could possibly have touched it.

The cistern-lever was pulled above her, again and again. Her nerve broke, and she rushed for the door. But the bolt wouldn't unbolt. Too stiff – too stiff for her terrified fingers. She flung herself round wildly, trying to climb over the top, but she was so terrified she couldn't manage that, either. She ended up cowering down against the door, head on her knees and hands over her ears, like an unborn baby.

Silence. Stillness. But she knew that whatever it was, it was still there.

'What . . . is . . . your . . . name?' she whispered, from a creaky throat. Then a shout. 'WHAT IS YOUR NAME?'

As if in answer, the toilet-roll began to unroll itself, rearing over her in swirling yellow coils, as if it wanted to smother her.

'Are you a spirit of health or goblin damned?' That reminded her of Dad, and gave her a little chip of courage. But the folds of paper went on rearing up, till all the cubicle was filled with the yellow, rustling mass. As if you had to *breathe* toilet paper.

'Begone . . . to the place . . . prepared for you,' she stammered, without hope. The coils of paper moved nearer, touching her face softly.

'WHAT DO YOU WANT?' She was screaming.

There was a change. The whirling folds of paper seemed to coalesce. Into a figure, taller than herself, as tall as a very thin boy might be, wrapped in yellow bands like a mummy, with two dark gaps where eyes might have been.

If it had touched her, her mind would have splintered into a thousand pieces.

But it didn't. It just looked at her, with its hole-eyes, and swung a yellow-swathed scarecrow arm to point to the brickwork above the cistern.

Three times. Till she dumbly nodded.

Then it collapsed into a mass of paper round her feet.

After a long time, she got up and tried the doorbolt. It opened easily, and her fear changed to embarrassment as she grabbed for her pants.

It hadn't wanted to harm her at all; it had only wanted to show her something.

Emboldened, she waded back through the yellow mass. Where had it been pointing?

There could be no mistake; a tiny strand of toilet-paper still clung to the brickwork, caught in a crack. She pulled it out, and the white paintwork crumbled a little and came with it, leaving a tiny hole. She touched the part near the hole, and more paint and cement crumbled; she scrabbled, and a whole half-brick seemed to fall out into her hand. Only it wasn't all brick, but crumbly dried mud, which broke and fell in crumbs all over the yellow paper.

What a mess! But left exposed was a square black hole, and there was something stuck inside. She reached in, and lifted down a thick bundle of papers . . .

Something made her lock the door, sit down on the toilet, and pull them out of their elastic band, which snapped with age as she touched it. Good heavens . . . her mouth dropped open, appalled.

There was a dusty passport; and a wallet. The wallet was full of money, notes. Pound notes and French thousand-franc notes. And a driving-licence, made out in the name of a Mr Alfred Barnett. And letters to Mr Barnett. And tickets for trains and a cross-channel ferry . . . and the passport, dated to expire on the first of April 1958, was also made out in the name of Alfred and Ada Barnett . . .

She sat there, and church-child that she was, she cried a little with relief and the pity of it. The ghost was a boy who had stolen and hidden the loot, so well concealed, all those years ago. And after he was dead, he was sorry, and wanted to make amends. But the school was abandoned by then; no-one to listen to him; old Crippen would never listen to a poor lost ghost . . . well, she would make amends for him, and then he would be at rest, poor lonely thing.

She looked at the address in the passport. 'Briardene', 12 Millbrook Gardens, Spilsby . . . why, it was only ten minutes' walk; she could do it on her way home tonight, and they wouldn't even worry about her getting home a bit late.

She was still sitting there in a happy and pious daze at the virtue of the universe, when faithful Vicky came looking for her. Only faithful Vicky had noticed she was gone. So she told her, and Vicky said she would come as well . . .

26

'They've taken Fiona to hospital . . .'

Perhaps that should have been a warning; but Rebeccah was too happy. 'She'll get over it; and once we've taken this, it won't hurt anybody else again.'

It all seemed so simple.

★   ★   ★

Liza came too; out of sheer nosiness, but Rebeccah was feeling charitable to all the world. It was that kind of blessed evening you sometimes get in January, lovely and bright, that makes you think of spring before the next snow falls.

Millbrook Gardens was in an older, solider district than their own; posher in its funny old way. Walls of brick that glowed a deep rich red in the setting sun, and showed their walking, blue girlish shadows, where there wasn't any ivy or the bare strands of Virginia Creeper. So it seemed that dim ghosts walked with them, among the houses with their white iron conservatories and old trees with homemade swings, and garden-seats still damp from winter. And funny stuffy names like 'Lynfield' and 'Spring Lodge' and 'Nevsky Villa'. It was hard to find 'Briardene' because there were no numbers on the houses. But they found it at last, looked over the gate and saw a snowy-haired, rosy-cheeked old man turning over the rose-beds in the big front garden.

He was quite a way from the gate; but he turned and looked at them. It wasn't a nice look; a long examining unfriendly look. They felt he didn't like children; they felt he would have liked to stop them coming in. But when Rebeccah called, in a too-shrill voice, 'Do Barnetts live here?' he abruptly waved them through to the front door, and went back to his digging. Rebeccah thought he must be the gardener; his clothes were quite old and shabby.

They trooped up to the front door, and rang. There was no answer for quite a long time, then the image of a plump, white-haired woman swam up the dark hall, all broken up by the stained-glass in the door.

She looked a bit friendlier than the gardener, but not much; full of an ancient suspicion and wariness.

'Yes, children?' she said, in an old-fashioned bossy way.

Rebeccah held out her dusty package, proudly. 'We found this – I think it's yours . . .'

The woman took it from her briskly enough; the way you take a parcel off a postman. But when she began to take off Rebeccah's new elastic band, she suddenly looked so . . . as if she'd like to drop the packet and slam the door.

'It's a passport and money and tickets and things,' said Rebeccah helpfully.

The woman put a hand to her eyes, to shield them as if the sunlight was too strong; she nearly fell, leaning against the door-post just in time. 'Alfred,' she called, 'Alfred!' to the man in the garden. Then Rebeccah knew the man was her husband, and she thought the cry was almost a call for help. As if they'd been attacking the woman . . .

The old man came hurrying up, full of petty anger at being disturbed. Until his wife handed him the packet. Then he too seemed to shrink, shrivel. The healthy high colour fled his cheeks, leaving only a pattern of bright broken veins, as if they'd been drawn on wrinkled fish-skin with a red Biro.

'They're . . .' said the woman.

'Yes,' said the man. Then he turned on the girls so fiercely they nearly ran away. His eyes were little and black and so full of hate that they, who had never been hit in their lives, grew afraid of being hit.

'*Where did you get these*?' There was authority in the voice, an ancient cruel utter authority . . .

'At Harvest Road School . . . I found them in the boys' toilets . . . hidden behind a whitewashed brick . . .'

'*Which toilet?*' The old man had grabbed Rebeccah with a terrible strength, by the shoulders; his fingers were savage. He began to shake her.

'Ey, watch it,' said Liza, aggressively. 'There's a law against that kind of thing.'

'I think we'll go now,' said Vicky frostily.

'*Which toilet?*'

'The far end one,' Rebeccah managed to gasp out. Staring into the old man's hot mad eyes, she was really frightened. This was not the way she'd meant things to go at all.

'*How* did you find it?' And, 'What were *you* doing there?'

'We're using the school . . . till ours is mended . . . we have to use the boys' toilets . . .'

'*Who* showed you?' Under his eyes, Rebeccah thought she was starting to fall to bits. Was he a lost member of the Gestapo, the Waffen SS? So she cried out, which she hadn't meant to,

'A *ghost* showed me – the ghost of a boy. It pointed to it . . .'

'That's right,' said Lisa, 'there *was* a ghost.' Stubbornly, loyally.

It worked; another terrible change came over the old man. All the cruel strength flowed out of his fingers. His face went whiter than ever. He staggered, and clutched at the windowsill to support himself. He began to breathe in a rather terrifying loud unnatural way.

'Help me get him in,' cried the woman. 'Help me get him in quick.'

Heaving and straining and panting and slithering on the dark polished floor, they got him through the hall and into a chintz armchair by the fire. He seemed to go unconscious. The woman went out, and came back with a tablet that she slipped into his mouth. He managed to swallow it. At first his breathing did not alter; then slowly it began to become more normal.

The woman seemed to come to herself; become aware of the little crowd, watching wide-eyed and gape-mouthed what they knew was a struggle between life and death.

'He'll be all right now,' she said doubtfully. 'You'd better be off home, children, before your mothers start to worry.' At the door she said, 'Thank you for bringing the things – I'm sure you thought you were doing your best.' She did not sound at all thankful really.

'We thought you'd better have them,' said Rebeccah politely. 'Even though they were so old . . .'

The woman looked sharply at her, as she heard the question in her voice. 'I suppose you'll want to tell your Headmistress what happened? You should have handed in the stuff to her, really . . . well, Mr Barnett was the last headmaster of Harvest Road – when it was boys, I mean – a secondary modern. It happened – those things were stolen on the last day of the summer term. We were going on holiday in France next day . . . we never went, we couldn't. My husband knew the boy who had stolen them, but he couldn't prove it. He had the school searched from top to bottom . . . the boy would admit nothing. It broke my husband's health . . . he resigned soon after, when the school had to close . . . good night, children. Thank you.'

She went as if to close the door on them, but Liza said sharply, 'Did the boys call your husband Barney Boko?'

The woman gave a slight but distinct shudder, though it could have been the cold January evening. 'Yes . . . they were cruel days, those, cruel.'

Then she closed the door quickly, leaving them standing there.

*　　*　　*

They hadn't gone fifty yards when Liza stopped them, grabbing each of them frantically by the arm, as if she was having a fit or something.

30

'Don't have it here,' said Vicky sharply. 'Wait till we get you to the hospital!'

But Liza didn't laugh. 'I remember now,' she said. 'Listen – my Dad went to that school – it was a terrible place. Barney Boko – Dad said he caned the kids for everything – even for spelling mistakes. The kids really hated him – some parents tried to go to the governors an' the council, but it didn't do any good. There was a boy called Stebbing – Barney Boko caned him once too often – he was found dead. I think it might have been in them toilets. The verdict was he fell – he had one of those thin skulls or something. They said he fell and banged his head.'

They stared at each other in horror.

'D'you think Stebbing's . . . what's in the toilets now?' asked Vicky.

They glanced round the empty streets; the lovely sun had vanished, and it had got dark awfully suddenly. There was a sudden rush coming at them round the corner – a ghostly rustling rush – but it was only long-dead autumn leaves, driven by the wind.

'Yes,' said Rebeccah, as calmly as she could. 'I think it was Stebbing. But he hasn't got anything against *us* – we did what he wanted.'

'What *did* he want?' asked Vicky.

'For me to take back what he'd stolen – to make up for the wrong he did.'

'You're too good for this world, Rebeccah!'

'What you mean?'

'Did Stebbing *feel* like he was sorry?' asked Vicky. 'Making Margie wet herself? Frightening Fiona into a fit? What he did to *you*?'

Rebeccah shuddered. 'He was angry . . .'

'What we have just seen,' said Vicky, 'is Stebbing's revenge . . .'

'How horrible. I don't believe that – it's too horrible . . .'

'He used you, ducky . . . boys will, if you let them . . .' Vicky sounded suddenly terribly bitter.

'Oh, I'm not going to listen. I'm going home.'

They parted in a bad silent mood with each other, though they stayed together as long as they could, through the windy streets, where the pools of light from the street-lights swayed. Rebeccah had the worst journey; she took her usual short-cut through the church-yard; before she'd realised what she'd done, she was halfway across and there was no point in turning back. She stood paralysed, staring at the teeth-like ranks of tombstones, that grinned at her in the faintest light of the last street-lamp.

Somewhere, among them, Stebbing must be buried. And the worst of it was, the oldest, Victorian grave-stones were behind her, and the newer ones in front. She could just make out the date on the nearest white one.

1956.

Stebbing must be very close.

She whimpered. Then she thought of God, who she really believed in. God wouldn't let Stebbing hurt her. She sort of reached out in her mind, to make sure God was there. In the windy night, He seemed very far away; but He *was* watching. Whimpering softly to herself, she walked on, trying not to look at the names on the tombstones, but not able to stop herself.

Stebbing was right by the path, third from the edge.

TO THE BELOVED MEMORY OF
BARRY STEBBING
BORN 11 MARCH 1944
DIED 22 JULY 1957
WITH GOD, WHICH IS MUCH BETTER

But Stebbing had nothing to say to her, here. Except, perhaps, a feeling it was all over, and his quarrel had never been with her. Really.

And then she was running, and the lights of home

were in front of her, and Stebbing far behind.

She burst into the front hall like a hurricane. Daddy always kept the outside front door open, and a welcoming light glowing through the inner one, even in the middle of winter.

Daddy was standing by the hallstand, looking at her. Wearing his dark grey overcoat, and carrying a little bag like a doctor's. Instinctively, as the child of the vicarage, she knew he was going to somebody who was dying.

'Oh,' she said, 'I wanted to talk to you.' All breathless.

He smiled, but from far away; as God had. He always seemed far away, when he was going to somebody who was dying.

'You'll have to wait, Person, I'm afraid. But I expect I'll be home for tea. And all the evening. The Church Aid meeting's been cancelled.'

'Oh, *good*.' Toast made at the fire, and Daddy, and a long warm evening with the curtains drawn against the dark . . .

'I wonder,' he said vaguely, 'can you help? Is Millbrook Gardens the second or third turn off Windsor Road? I can never remember . . .'

'Second from the bottom.' Then, in a rush, 'Who's dying?'

He smiled, puzzled. They never talked about such things. 'Just an old man called Barnett . . . heart giving out. But his wife says he's very troubled . . . wants to talk about something he did years ago that's on his mind. I'd better be off, Rebeccah. See you soon.' He went out. She heard his footsteps fading down the path.

She clutched the hallstand desperately, her eyes screwed tight shut, so she wouldn't see her face in the mirror.

'Come home soon, Daddy,' she prayed. 'Come home soon.'

Wing Quack Flap

by

Joan Aiken

'It really *can't* be a healthy situation,' repeated the Welfare Officer nervously. Her name was Miss Wenban; she was thin and pretty, with curly dark hair and a pink-and-white complexion; she came from the South and had not yet grown accustomed to tough Northern ways and the bleakness of Northern landscapes.

'Healthy? Fadge! It's healthy enow!' snarled Grandfather.

Every utterance of Grandfather's came out as a snarl, partly because of the shape of his mouth, which was wide and thin like the slot in a money-box; it seemed meant for putting things in, not for words coming out. And indeed, while Grandfather ate his meals, grimly and speedily shovelling in hot-pot, oatcakes, porridge, or kippers, he always insisted on silence.

'Eat your vittles and shurrup, boy! Mealtimes is meant for eating, not for gabbing. Hold your tongue and gan on with your grub.'

Pat, whose father had been Irish and talkative, could remember mealtimes at home in Manchester when the three of them, he and Da and Ma, had had so much to say to one another, arguing and joking and laughing, that the food had grown cold on their plates; and not because it was tasteless food, either; Ma had been a prime cook; but that was long ago now.

Years ago it seemed, and was; three whole years.

Not that Aunt Lucy wasn't a good cook too. Ma's only sister: it would be funny if she weren't. Ma had been little and pretty and round, like a bird; Aunt Lucy wasn't very like her in other ways. But she really seemed to put her soul into her cooking, Pat thought; that, and trying to keep the cottage as tidy and clean as circumstances would allow. Aunt Lucy's soul didn't seem to come out in anything else she did: wan, silent and bedraggled, small and grey as the ghost of an otter, with bulging bloodshot scared eyes and flat, scraped-back hair, she crept about the house in a faded cotton overall and fabric slippers with the toes gone out of them. She winced nervously at Grandfather's thumps and shouts, although she had lived with them forty-eight years; and, as long as Grandfather was in the house, she spoke as seldom as possible.

Once, unexpectedly, she had said to Pat, 'I can remember when cowslips grew on Kelloe Bank.'

'And what if you can?' snarled Grandfather. 'What's so remarkable about *that*? You going to sit down and write a letter to the *Northern Echo* about that?'

Aunt Lucy winced and trembled, sank her thin neck down between her shoulders, and went back to separating currants for lardy cake. She had never been able to master reading and writing; it was a sensitive point with her, and Grandfather often referred to her disability, using it as a punishment, either for her or for Pat, whichever of them at that moment had exasperated him. If Pat had a bad report from school – which, luckily, was rare – or did something that annoyed Grandfather – which was much more likely to happen – Aunt Lucy was the one who always came in for the first blast of his ire.

'Hah! I can see you're going to grow up like your daft aunt there. No use to a man or beast. Two of ye; what a prospect. Thank the lord *I* shan't be around to have the job of looking after ye. Thank the lord I'll be under-ground.'

However it didn't seem probable that Grandfather

would be underground for a long time yet; not long past his mid sixties, he was hale and stringy as an old root. His coarse white hair stood up on end, thick as marsh grass; out of his red, wind-chapped face – which was only shaved twice a week, sprouted over with grizzled black-and-white stubble the rest of the time – glared two small angry pale-grey eyes, always on the look-out for trouble. Grandfather was in a rage about having been compulsorily retired from his job in the Council Roads Department; he was in a rage about the death of his daughter Sue, Pat's mother, and her husband Micky, in a flu epidemic; he was in a rage about the price of tobacco, and about Stockton United having been beaten by Middlesbrough; the only thing that did not put Grandfather in a rage, oddly enough, was the situation in which he, Aunt Lucy, and young Pat were obliged to live.

This situation was why the Welfare Officer came calling so often. But Grandfather had taken up a rock-hard position about it, from which he would not be budged.

'No. No. *No*! I don't intend to leave this cottage. I was born here – and so was *my* granddad – and they're not getting me out of here till they carry me feet first. After that, they can do as they damn please – I don't care what they do with the place, they can blow it up if they like.'

They would never do that, though. The little house itself was protected by all kinds of Acts of Parliament. It was listed and scheduled and selected for preservation because a building had always stood there on that site from way back, mentioned in Domesday Book if not earlier, and also because it was one of the very earliest examples of a weaver's cottage, and still had the loom, on which Grandfather's Granda had woven, in the back room. A great nuisance the loom was; Pat often longed to take a hatchet to it. Then he could have had a room of his own, instead of being obliged to sleep on the settee in the front room. Also the back room would have been less noisy, though damper than the front, being built into the side of the hill.

It was the location of the house, Kelloe Bank Cottage it was called, that caused Welfare Visitors to write pages of notes, and Medical Officers to make continual reports to Health Committees.

Kelloe Bank Cottage stood, as its name suggested, halfway up a steep, an almost vertical bank, directly between the concrete legs that carried one monstrous motorway, and looking down at another, which circled the foot of the bank, so that all day, and all night too, a thundering, grinding, roaring, oil-exuding, dust-hurling torrent of cars, trucks, tankers, and vans poured to and fro, to and fro, above and below.

The Welfare Visitors and Health Officers often found it difficult to hear or to make themselves heard above the din of the traffic; they tended to stagger away after their visits shaking with strain, and gulping down headache pills; but Grandfather and Aunt Lucy seemed to have developed an ability to hear normal sounds above the roar of motors, and so, after a year or two, did Pat; but then he began to suffer from a lot of bad sore throats and coughs.

That was why Miss Wenban was here again. Once more she had braved the approach to the cottage, which was not an easy one. You had to leave your car in the layby on the road on the south side of the east-west motorway down below, climb over a stile, scramble down the embankment, and then trudge along a nasty squelchy footpath which ran through a tunnel under the motorway; emerging on the northern side, you scrabbled your way up an even steeper track to the cottage, whose tidily kept garden, with rows of leeks and cabbages, hung down before it like a striped apron spread over the hillside. Another path led round the cottage and upward from the rear, right under the massive legs of the north-south motorway, and so on up Kelloe Bank; but you could not get very far that way, for the top of the ridge was ruled across, like the seam on a football, by a tremendous barbed-wire fence and a row of mighty pylons, guarded with DANGER signs; beyond that, the other side of the hill was the property of Kelloe Bank Generating Station, and eight huge cooling-towers stood in a group like giants' pepper-pots, blocking the access to the plain.

Aunt Lucy believed the cooling towers leaked electricity.

'You can feel it in the air, often; and you can hear it ticking,' she whispered confidentially to Miss Wenban. Grandfather, in a rage with what he called 'Women's clack', had gone out, muttering venomous things under his breath, and was hoeing between the rows of vegetables, or Lucy would never have found the courage to speak.

With her trembling little claw hands she took hold of Miss Wenban's arm.

'Sometimes you can hear the air tick, like the sound of a spider making its web; other times it's more like a lark singing, or the hum of a bee. When it ticks, I'm scared to strike a match, in case the spark sets off the whole house.'

'It's the exhaust fumes that bother *me*,' said Miss Wenban, looking at Aunt Lucy rather hopelessly. Then she nibbled the delicious crumbly, buttery wedge of parkin, and sipped the hot fresh cup of tea that Aunt Lucy had set by her on a small tin tray painted with lilies-of-the-valley. 'I worry about all the carbon monoxide that must be pouring into your lungs – this is no place for you to live.'

'Dad won't ever, ever shift from this cottage,' whispered Aunt Lucy. 'And I don't see how we could manage without him. He does all the shopping, you see, in

Coalshiels; I never go out any more; I haven't left the house in twenty years.'

'Why not?'

'Dad thinks, better not. I might get lost. It's all so different now from when I was a girl.'

'I could take you about, Auntie,' offered Pat. 'Or I could do the shopping, on my way home from school.'

The yellow school bus stopped for Pat every morning, pulling into the layby, and brought him back at tea time; on the days when he was well enough to go to school.

'Four and a half weeks you've missed this term, Pat,' said Miss Wenban. 'That's awful, you know, in a nine-week term; it's half your education gone.'

'I'm sorry,' croaked Pat, and he was. 'It isn't that I don't like school. And I read when I'm at home, books from the school library. It's my bad throats.'

'Is it bad now? Open your mouth. Yes, I can see it is.'

Miss Wenban was bothered, also, by the fact that Pat could not bring friends home.

'I have friends at school, all right,' he assured her. 'But their parents won't let them come here. Too dangerous. It'd mean biking along the main road in all that traffic.'

'Nowt to stop 'em coming over the water-meadows, the way I go to get the vittles,' growled Grandfather, who had been driven back indoors by a heavy shower. You couldn't hear the rain, because of the traffic roar, but you could see rivulets of water making clean lines on the exhaust-grimed windows. 'Mind, I'm not complaining,' Grandfather added. 'Who wants a passel of young 'uns about the place? Not I? *One*'s bad enow.' He directed a scowl at Pat, which made Miss Wenban say firmly,

'Pat ought to have company. It's not good for a lad always to be with his elders.'

Specially when one of them's a bit simple, Pat could see her thinking, though she was too tactful to say it.

In Pat's view, Aunt Lucy was not daft. Just scared off balance by Grandfather, was the conclusion he had come to; otherwise she was sensible enough, when you got her on her own. If it weren't for the horribleness of Da and Ma dying, Pat often thought it was a lucky thing for Aunt Lucy that he had come to live at Kelloe Bank Cottage; since his arrival she had brightened up a bit, and they had tiny secrets together when Grandfather was out of the way, over swallows' nests and butterflies and things Pat told her about school.

'I suppose you can't have radio or TV here under the viaduct –' went on Miss Wenban.

'Who wants that trash? Pack o' rubbish!' snorted Grandfather.

'– But if Pat could keep a pet, now? A – kitten, or a budgerigar?'

'And isn't *that* just like women's fimble-famble?' burst out Grandfather with utter scorn. 'Why would giving the boy a *kitten* cure his sore throat? Any road, I won't have a bird twitterin' and messin' about the house. That I tell you straight! Nor a cat, either.'

Pat said nothing. He had once *had* a kitten, a little black-and-white cat named Whisky, brought with him when he came to Kelloe Bank Cottage from Manchester. Grandfather had thrown Whisky out, one rainy night, in order to punish Pat for what he called 'sulks and whinges'; Pat still held his mind well away from the memory of Whisky's end, flattened under the wheels of a petrol-tanker.

'Just the same, you should have something. What kind of a pet could you keep here? Perhaps a goldfish?'

Miss Wenban was not going to let Grandfather put her down.

'I don't think I'd want a goldfish, thank you,' croaked Pat politely.

41

'Oh. Um.' Miss Wenban was momentarily at a standstill. 'Well, I shall think about it and come up with some other suggestions next week,' and she left before Grandfather could sneer or snarl any more, edging her way through heavy rain down the steep track. Pat watched her with concern through the rain-washed window; he liked Miss Wenban and understood that she meant kindly by him and Aunt Lucy, though her visits tended to bring them much more trouble than if she had stayed away.

'Nearly went tail over tip *that* time,' commented Grandfather, watching with a sour grin as the Welfare Visitor slid, and just managed to recover her balance. 'It'd be a right laugh if she slipped down the bank and went under a truck. Mayhap then the rest of 'em wouldn't be so keen to come pestering us, nosyparkering in what's none o' their ruddy business. And as for *you* – *you* just lick her boots!' he grated out, rounding on Lucy. 'Wha'd'you want to go feeding her tea an' parkin for? Who told you to do that?'

Poor Lucy started with terror and dropped a plate on the stone floor. Luckily it was only an enamel plate, but a chip flew off and Grandfather stormed at her.

'Now look what you've done! Blubberfingers!'

Fortunately at that moment he noticed that the rain had eased off, and so he went out to resume his garden work.

Lucy rubbed her thumb over the chipped enamel, sucked in her breath, and gave Pat a nervous fluttering smile. She had gone red and white in patches, all over her face, as she mostly did when Grandfather shouted at her.

'Never mind, Aunt Lucy,' Pat comforted her. 'April's nearly here. Soon Grandfather will be out of doors most of the day. And your chilblains will get better. And my sore throats usually stop in April. Let's have a nibble of parkin,' he went on, trying to cheer her, though he found it hard to swallow. 'It's grand – the best you ever made.'

But Aunt Lucy was struggling to say something.

'A pet – Miss Wenban – she say you ought to have a pet –'

'Nah,' Pat told her quickly. 'I don't *want* a pet. It – it just wouldn't do here – not with Grandfather and all –'

Aunt Lucy nodded a great many times, very rapidly, with fluttering eyelids.

'When I was a gal – had a collie dog – Lassie –' she whispered presently. 'Your Uncle Frank – got her for me – time he went to sea.'

Pat nodded. Letters from Uncle Frank arrived from places like Hong Kong and Sydney and Recife and Bombay; Uncle Frank, in the merchant navy, was a great traveller. And sounded a kind man.

'Your Granda – never did like Lassie,' Aunt Lucy whispered. 'Didn't like her at all.' Pat nodded again. He could easily guess the kind of thing that had happened to Lassie. He put an arm round Aunt Lucy and hugged her.

'Never mind, Auntie! Who wants an old pet that's always needing its water changed, or its sand-tray emptied?'

Then Aunt Lucy surprised him.

'Got a pet! You – you can share her.'

'*You've* got a pet, Aunt Lucy?'

Pat stared around the familiar little front room in bewilderment. Was Aunt Lucy really a bit daft, a bit touched in her wits? He studied the grimy windows, the lace curtains that Aunt Lucy did her best to keep clean, the grubby red inner curtains, the shabby settee, the table with red chenille cloth matching the curtains, three wooden chairs, dresser with plates and pots, mantelshelf with clock and matches, fireplace with built-in oven; on the walls, two pictures of the sea and a calendar with a windmill; on the high shelf a lustre cup ('A Present from

Scarborough') and a Chinese teapot, a present from Uncle Frank. Twice he let his eyes roam all round the room. Upstairs, Aunt Lucy's room contained no more than bed, chair, clothes-hook on the back of the door, and window. Well, he decided, it's just a bit of her fancy, like the electricity leaking from the cooling-towers. I won't fuss her about it.

Aloud, he said, 'Can I have a bit more hot in this cup, Aunt Lucy? I let it get cold while Miss Wenban was here.'

She poured him half a cupful from the old brown pot; it was still hot, and he drank it in slow, careful sips, letting it slide gently down his sore throat. Doing so, he allowed his eyes to slip out of focus, so that he was able to see two blue teacups and three brown segments of tea, two pointing to right and left, a joined one meeting in the middle of his nose.

'Chinese duck's my pet!' whispered Aunt Lucy, with a triumphant smile. Her face for a moment was quite bright and lively, reminded him of Ma. But don't think of Ma, don't, don't, don't. Aunt Lucy went on, 'I keep her in Uncle Frank's teapot. Name's Wing Quack Flap.' She nodded and smiled and said again, 'You can share her.'

Pat nearly choked on his tea. Gulping down the last mouthful he set his cup carefully back on the saucer, while his eyes winked back into focus. But – astonishingly – just before they did so, he could have sworn that he saw a beautiful shining duck, a mandarin duck, fly across the room. The duck was transparent, ghostly, it was like the double images that he had seen when his eyes were out of focus. Through its colours he could see the brown pattern of the wallpaper behind. But the colours were brilliant – red, pink, snowy white, deep blue, dark, lustrous green. The duck circled the room once, at speed, then vanished inside Uncle Frank's Chinese teapot – which was far, far too small to contain the bird that had flown into it. There could not possibly have been enough room inside. Besides, the lid was on.

'I'm going barmy too,' Pat thought. 'Head aches. Better take an aspirin.'

'Wing Quack Flap,' whispered Aunt Lucy again, with that quick, twitching smile, her bulgy eyes flitting towards the window, outside which Grandfather could be heard digging and grunting. Then she took the brown teapot to empty the swillings outside.

While she was out, Pat climbed on one of the chairs, lifted down the Chinese teapot, and looked inside. As he had expected, there was nothing. He carefully put it back, and then, somehow, he must have slipped, for the next thing he knew was that he was lying on the floor, and Aunt Lucy was clucking and exclaiming over him.

'I feel a bit queer, Aunt Lucy,' he croaked . . .

*   *   *

The fact that Pat was tucked up on the sofa having flu made no difference at all to the habits of Grandfather, who stomped in and out as usual, gnashing and growling. But fortunately the weather had taken a turn for the better, and at this season Grandfather was a dedicated gardener; he was out of the house more than he was indoors, hoeing, trenching, sowing, transplanting and mulching all day, while the traffic boomed and howled and fumed above and below him.

Pat could have his flu in peace, with Aunt Lucy and Wing Quack Flap to keep him company.

Aunt Lucy brewed innumerable hot drinks, which were all that Pat could keep down; Wing Quack Flap soared and swooped overhead, keeping him endlessly amused with her effortless aerobatics. Ninety per cent of the time she was airborne; she hardly ever alighted. Sometimes she flew through into the back room, if the door was open, and perched on the loom. Just occasionally she would come to rest on the red chenille

45

tablecloth. When she did come to a stop, what charmed Pat even more than her brilliant colours was her friendly goodhumoured expression. She was a little like Ma – always looked as if she were just about to break into a laugh. Very different from Grandfather! Her rosy bill curved in a permanent smile, her orange webbed feet turned out at a carefree angle, her black eyes twinkled with humour and knowingness. She shone in the dark little house where, despite Aunt Lucy's best efforts, everything was worn, everything was grimy and shabby from the exhaust fumes and dust that poured round the windowframes and under the door and through the curtains. But Wing Quack Flap was not grimy: she was shining and glossy like a new horse-chestnut just popped from its rind.

For the first day or two she was silent; but as Pat's flu took hold of him she began to quack: at the start, a comfortable contented gobbling noise, of the kind that ducks make when they are dabbling with their bills through muddy, weedy water: griddle graddle, griddle graddle, griddle graddle. Then, by and by, as she flew, she brought out a loud joyful honking quack: WAAARK, wark-wark-wark-wark-wark. Pat could hear it easily above the sound of the traffic, and he thought it quite the nicest noise he had heard since the days when his father used to sing 'Peg in a low-backed car' and other Irish songs. Often Pat fell asleep to the sound of Wing Quack Flap's conversation.

'But, Aunt Lucy – is it right to keep her in the teapot?' he muttered one day, between temperatures, when Grandfather was out doing the shopping at Coalshiels Co-op. 'The pot's too small for her.'

'Nowhere else to put her. Nowhere that's safe,' said Aunt Lucy.

There came a day when Pat's flu rose up like a river in spate and nearly swamped him entirely; when light and dark fled past one another in a flickering, speeding race like the headlights of the traffic along the two motorways; when Pat's thumping heart and his drawing, dragging breath made such a deal of noise that he was unable to hear the trucks and tankers above and below; when Doctor Dilip Rao came from Coalshiels, and a nurse in dark blue and brass buttons from Hutton End; when there was talk about an ambulance and hospital; only, they were saying to each other, how could they manage to carry a stretcher up the steep slippery path, let alone through the narrow tunnel under the Hawtonstall Highway?

In the middle of their argument Pat sat up in bed, watching the zigzags of Wing Quack Flap, who was in the back room playing Follow-my-leader with herself in and out of great-grandfather's loom.

'I'd rather stay at home,' he announced. 'I'd rather stay with Aunt Lucy and Wing Quack Flap.'

No one paid any heed to his actual words: they were all so startled to see him sit up and act like a human being.

'Peck o' silly chatteration, talk o' fetching the boy to hospital,' growled Grandfather, stumping in out of the garden. 'Nowt ails the lad but a touch o' grip; and that's on its way out. Young 'uns weren't molly-coddled in hospital when *I* were a lad; you stayed home an' got better by yoursen.' He scowled at Doctor Dilip.

'Well –' said the doctor. 'In view of the difficulty with the ambulance –' He glanced at Nurse Enderby.

'I'll come in again this afternoon,' she promised. 'And first thing tomorrow.'

Aunt Lucy said nothing at all but looked nervously from one to the other. While the doctor examined Pat she had taken Nurse Enderby into the back room and held a conversation with her, pressed up against the loom. Now Lucy was kneading and wringing her hands as if she rolled a strip of lardy-cake dough on a floured board. And if anyone had stood close beside her, they

47

might have heard her whisper, 'It isn't right, it isn't right, it isn't right!'

Dr Dilip and Nurse Enderby left, and Pat let himself slip down under the covers again. He felt tired and giddy from so much company.

'I'll make that call for you,' murmured the nurse to Aunt Lucy on her way out. Luckily Grandfather did not hear.

'Beef tea – put on a kettle – make a cup of hot –' fluttered Aunt Lucy, and took the brown jug from the dresser and went out to the tap at the side of the cottage.

'Now those daft pokenoses have left,' snarled Grandfather, suddenly rounding with unexpected savagery on Pat as he lay limp under the blanket of knitted squares – 'now *they're* out of the road, what was that I heard you say about your Aunt Lucy and some rubbish?'

Pat felt weak and hopeless. He could not protect himself from Grandfather's little grey gimlet eyes, which bored into Pat like laser beams, and his grating, angry voice which demanded again,

'What was that I heard you say? Quack quack flip flap – or something daft?'

'Wing Quack Flap is *not* daft!' feverishly flung back Pat. 'She's not daft – she's our duck – our beautiful duck – and she lives in the Chinese teapot –'

'*What* did you say? I'll give you Chinese teapot, my lad!' roared Grandfather. 'I'm not having *you* grow up ninepence-in-the-shilling, like your sawney aunt! I'm stopping any such nonsense *now* – once and for all. Wing Quack Flap, indeed! I twisted *that* perishing bird's neck twenty years ago, and all! I'll have no more of it now!'

And he strode across to where he could reach the high shelf, stretched up, and seized hold of the Chinese teapot.

'Wait, you, till I get this window open – Wing Quack Flap, indeed!'

'Grandfather. *No!*' cried Pat in agony.

But Grandfather, with a great swing back of his arm, had hurled the teapot out through the open window — flung it so hard and savagely that Pat, waiting for the crash against the garden wall, heard, instead, a shriek of brakes down below on the motorway, and then the tinkle of smashed glass, and shouts, and horns blaring.

– 'What in the *world* is going on in here?' demanded Miss Wenban the Welfare Visitor, walking into the room just at that moment.

*   *   *

Grandfather had been taken down to the police station to be charged. Not with manslaughter – mercifully for him, in the pile-up caused when the teapot he had thrown out went through the windscreen of an articulated car-transporter, although numerous people were hurt, and thousands of pounds' worth of damage had been done, nobody had actually died. But when the police came up to the cottage Grandfather had flown into such a passion and resisted arrest so ferociously that he was now in a cell and would probably remain there for some days. But that was all right, for Uncle Frank was flying home from Naples, where Nurse Enderby had managed to contact him by radio telephone.

'He says he was thinking of retiring this year in any case,' Nurse Enderby told Aunt Lucy and Pat. '– Thank you, Miss Blackhall, I wouldn't say no to another cup of tea, and a sliver of that lardy-cake. Your brother said he had it in mind to start a little baker's shop, in Tunstall, and maybe you and the boy could live with him there.'

'Then Granda can stay here on his own,' said Pat, comfortably leaning back on his sagging heap of cushions. 'He'll like that better than having us.'

Aunt Lucy nodded several times without speaking. But her eyes shone brighter than they had for months.

After Nurse Enderby had gone Pat said sadly, 'I'm sorry – I'm very sorry about – about your teapot, Aunt

Lucy. It was all my fault. I shouldn't have said anything to Grandfather. And I'm sorry about –'

The name stuck in his throat. Already he was beginning to wonder if Wing Quack Flap had existed at all, in any way – or had she simply been part of his illness? Had he made up the whole thing?

But Aunt Lucy, nodding over and over, wide-eyed, solemn, patted his hand several times and whispered, 'Never mind, never mind! Can't be helped. Besides – you were right. Teapot not big enough. No! But listen now – listen!'

Shaking her head, muttering scoldingly to herself, she pattered away to the window and opened it wide. 'Not too cold now. Listen!' she said again. 'Listen, Pat!'

Outside, April twilight was thickening, and though the traffic roar could still be heard, at this time of the evening the noise had diminished a little; indeed, as Aunt Lucy stood by the casement, her finger conspiratorially to her lips, a brief lull came, in which no vehicle passed on either highway, above or below.

And during that lull something else would be heard instead: a loud series of triumphant honking quacks: WAAARK, WAAARK, WAAARK, wark-wark-wark-wark-wark. Round and round the house the cry circled, three, four, five, six times; then, fading away, it receded into the far distance.

Back to China, perhaps, thought Pat.

Soon the traffic roar began again.

My Mother's Story

by

Antonia Barber

The strange events in this story happened to my mother when she was a young girl. She was much the same age as you are now, a slim, solemn girl with large dark eyes who looks out at me from the old photographs in our family album.

Here she is as a child and underneath in fine copper-plate handwriting 'Beatrice aged 6, Lily aged 4'. Lily is all curls and a frilly frock: she is clutching a splendid doll which belonged to the photographer and there is a triumphant smile on her plump little face. Beatrice, my mother, looks sulky and cross: she had also wanted to hold the doll but 'frilly Lily' had a knack of getting her own way.

In the next picture, baby Frederick has put in an appearance, held proudly on my grandmother's knee. Lily is in the foreground spreading the skirt of her frock in an effort to hog as much of the picture as possible. My grandfather stands tall in his uniform for this is the time of the first world war. Beatrice? Oh yes, there she is, you can just see her face in that dark corner, looking over her mother's shoulder.

My grandfather was one of the lucky ones who survived the war, if you can call them 'lucky' coming back to unemployment and hardship. He managed to find a job but only by working late into the night for a miserable wage. So the arrival of another child, my Uncle Edward, was a very mixed blessing and is recorded only in a faded snapshot taken on the front steps of the house.

But it is an interesting picture, for this is the house where it happened. It looks ordinary enough, a typical suburban London house built at the turn of the century: one of a terrace with semi-basement, bay window, and a short flight of steps leading up to the front doorway where the family are posing.

My grandfather is smiling: he was a cheerful man and probably grateful just to be alive. My grandmother, clutching baby Edward, looks pale and worried, as well she might with four children to feed. Fred is about five, the image of his father even to the grin on his mischievous face: Lily is smirking as usual and Beatrice is smouldering in the background. Her dark eyes are larger than ever and smudged underneath with circles of sleeplessness. Was it the baby's crying or was it the house itself that kept her awake through the long hours of the night? But perhaps I am letting my imagination run away with me, for my mother said this picture was taken soon after they moved in, before anything actually happened.

The man from the house agent had shown them around, sliding up the sash windows to prove that they did not stick. They did, so he shut them hastily and pointed out the 'elegant' cast iron mantelpiece. 'And you've got a handy little nursery here,' he lied, throwing open the door of a small boxroom and closing it again quickly before they could see quite how small it was.

'What do you think?' asked my grandfather.

'It's cheap,' said my grandmother who could see nothing else to recommend it.

'It's got a garden!' chorused Lily and Fred, flattening their noses against the rear window to admire the overgrown tangle of weeds beyond.

'I don't like it: it feels strange,' said Beatrice gloomily.

'Speak when you're asked,' said her father shortly: he could do without her fads and fancies. 'What do you think, Jess?' he asked again.

'We'll take it,' said my grandmother, for it was half the price of the flat they were leaving.

They moved in and at first things seemed ordinary enough. They were so crowded together and Lily and Fred made so much noise that it was hard to imagine anything strange or mysterious about the house. The baby fretted at night, but babies often do. My grandmother, Jess, found it hard to sleep but was that surprising with all her worries and the baby wakeful? Only Beatrice actually complained about the house, but her mother, driven out of patience by the antics of Lily and Fred, cuffed her soundly and told her to keep her moans to herself.

'There's no satisfying you, Beatie,' she said. 'Be grateful for a roof over your head.'

Beatie could not have explained why the house made her so uneasy. She would lie awake at night listening to the footsteps going down the stairs and the back of her neck would prickle.

'Ma,' she asked one day, 'why does the old man go downstairs at night?'

'Don't ask me,' said Jess, up to her elbows in flour and suet. 'I've enough to do without poking my nose into other people's affairs . . . And, anyway, how do you know what he does at night? You're supposed to be asleep.'

'I hear him every night going down the stairs,' said Beatie.

'I expect you imagine it,' said her mother.

'Edward hears him too,' said Beatie.

'O-ooh, what a lie!' said Lily prissing up her mouth into a round O of disapproval. 'You can't possibly know what Edward hears because he can't talk . . . and that makes you a liar, Beatie Gordon!'

She shrieked and ran as Beatie came lunging at her with fists flying. Jess sprang to separate them, dealing out stinging slaps which sent the flour flying in clouds about them. 'Don't call your sister a liar, Lily,' she chided angrily.

'But, Ma, how does she know what Edward hears?'

'I know because he always wakes up!' shouted Beatie furiously. 'Whenever the old man goes downstairs, Eddie wakes up and cries and that wakes Ma. If the old man stopped going downstairs at night, Ma could get some sleep!' She loved her mother dearly in spite of the knowledge that Lily was her favourite. It worried her to see the pinched face and the tired eyes.

'Well, there's some sense in that,' said Jess, pushing back her hair with a hand that left white smudges on her forehead. 'Perhaps I'll have a word with the old man.'

It was on the following day that Beatie was left alone in the house for the first time. As a rule, Jess took them all with her when she went shopping and stopped in the park for an hour on the way home. But on this occasion Beatie was in disgrace, having been caught with both hands locked into Lily's hair apparently trying to pull it out by the roots. If the truth must be told that is exactly what she was trying to do, driven beyond bearing by yet another disparaging comparison from Lily between her own blonde curls and Beatie's straight dark 'rat's tails'. 'Well, let's see how you look when you're *bald*!' Beatie had shouted, descending upon the maddening golden halo like a bat out of hell.

And now she was on her own, lips pursed in the stubborn anger which had made her miss the longed-for outing rather than say she was sorry. She watched from the window as her mother bumped the pram down the front steps followed by Fred and the tear-streaked Lily, who turned as she went to put out her tongue in a gesture of triumph.

It was only when their chattering voices passed out of earshot, and silence descended like a blanket around her, that Beatie realised she was *not* alone. It was not a vague feeling, you understand, but an absolute conviction, so that she was afraid to turn and look behind her for fear of what she might see. She stood without moving, feeling the beat of her heart as it began to race, still staring out into the empty street. There was a distinct coldness behind her. She tried to reassure herself that it was the sunlight, shining on her face and hands, that made her back feel so cold . . . but she knew that it was not true. Only minutes before her mother had remarked how hot and stuffy the room was, trying to persuade Beatie to apologise and go with them. Now the coldness was growing, rubbing itself against the back of her neck, like the cold cloth Jess laid there when Beatie had one of her headaches. She had a sudden desperate need to make contact with the sunlit street outside: leaning forward she sprang the catch and heaved at the sash window, but it would not move. Panicking, she turned to one of the side windows of the bay only to find that the changed angle and the dark foliage of a stunted tree outside reflected back her own frightened face . . . and another face beside her own.

With a shriek of pure terror she spun round, preferring whatever she might find within the room to that ghostly image in the dim glass of the window.

But there was nothing there: only the coldness which moved away from her like a physical presence. Frantic, she rushed to the door, through the hall with its cool mosaic tiled floor and out on to the reassuringly hot and dusty front steps. Here she sat for the next hour, squinting uncomfortably into the bright sunlight, trying to get what shade she could from the stunted tree, preferring any discomfort to the unknown presence in the house behind her. Whatever it is, she told herself, it can't get me out here.

Then just when she had begun to feel normal again, when the memory of the panic had begun to fade, she heard footsteps coming down the stairs inside and her heart began to pound again. They were slow, dragging

footsteps, like some creature moving in great pain. Step
. . . after step . . . after step, they drew inexorably closer
to the front door where she sat. Beatie was up like a shot
and down the overgrown steps that wound sideways
into the basement area. From here she watched with
wide-eyed horror as the front door creaked slowly open
. . . and then the old man from upstairs came out. Relief
flooded her and she crouched among the rank weeds
feeling very foolish and hoping he would not notice her.
He turned to close the door and then came on down
taking his weight on a stick to spare a lame leg.

As Beatrice watched his slow progress along the street,
she saw Jess and the children returning, saw her mother
pause to speak to the old man, remembered her decision
to have a word with him. But Beatie already knew
before she saw him shake his head, that it was not the
old man whose footsteps she heard: it was not the lame
tread that came so lightly downstairs in the night. A
sudden thought struck her: she had only ever heard the
footsteps coming down: they never went up again . . .
But there was no time to pursue the memory, barely
time to get back indoors before Lily's eagle eye could
spot her and draw her mother's attention to this new
disobedience. For Beatie had been given strict instruc-
tions to serve out her punishment indoors.

'I spoke to the old man,' said Jess, unpacking the
groceries from the well of the pram. 'He never goes
downstairs at night.'

'I know,' said Beatie, undoing a plain blue bag of sugar
and sticking her finger in. 'It's not him: he limps; the
footsteps don't.' She put the sugary finger in her mouth
and licked off the clinging grains. Jess slapped the back
of her hand as she reached to do it again.

'Well, then you must have imagined it, and *don't do
that*, Beatie, I've told you a hundred times.'

And there it rested for a while. Beatie made sure she
was never in the house alone: she saved her rows with

Lily until after they got back from the park. And once she began to listen for the footsteps, she seemed to fall asleep before she heard them. The baby still woke and cried, but that did not seem to prove anything.

Then one day Jess announced that she had taken an evening job at a local cinema. 'We need the money, so you'll have to mind the others while I'm out,' she told Beatie firmly. 'You're old enough to make yourself useful. I'll fix your tea before I go and I shall be home about half-past ten.'

It was Lily who raised the wildest moan, appalled by the idea of Beatie in charge and free to avenge all the slights of the day. Beatie, on the other hand, was quite made up with the idea. After all, she thought, I shan't be alone with Lily and Fred and the baby to take charge of. Nevertheless she had a sudden sense of being abandoned to her fate when Jess locked the door of the flat firmly behind her and vanished down the steps into the lamp-studded darkness.

'Right,' she said turning upon Lily, 'you're to go to bed an hour early for calling me names this afternoon.'

'Who said I was calling you names?' protested Lily. 'I just happened to say "Uglybug". I suppose a person can say "Uglybug" if they feel like it without it being a crime. Who said I was talking to you? I mean if the cap fits . . .'

But these finer points of logic were lost on Beatie, temporarily drunk with power. 'An hour early,' she said heartlessly, and when Lily began to moan she added, 'You know what Ma said: anyone who plays me up can't go to the park, and if you stay in the house alone, the dreaded ghost will get you.'

'Which dreaded ghost?' Lily stopped in her tracks and Fred was suddenly all ears, so Beatie told them a highly coloured version of her uncanny experience.

'You're telling lies again!' Lily forgot her vulnerable position in her anxiety to disprove the frightening apparition. She felt she would never dare to look into her mirror again and it was one of her favourite pastimes.

'Don't call me a liar, Lily Gordon!' shouted Beatie indignantly, and she did after all have justice on her side. 'I did see a ghost, so you can jolly well go to bed two hours early which is right now!' And the protesting Lily was sent off with Fred who was due for bed anyway and delighted to have company.

The three children slept together in a big bed in the 'nursery' boxroom, while Eddie had his cot alongside his parents' bed. The three rooms lay one behind the other: living-room at the front, a door leading into the bedroom, and the boxroom leading out of that. Once she had packed Lily and Fred off to bed and popped Edward into his cot, Beatie found she was on her own.

The companionable television set had not yet been invented, and if the wireless had put in an appearance, it had not reached the homes of the poor. Beatie sat, trying to enjoy the luxury of having the living-room to herself, with no sound but the pop and flare of the gas light to break the silence. The faint sound of giggling and squeaking that reached her from the distant box-room, only made her feel more alone.

Then the baby began to cry.

Beatie went in to comfort him and to grumble at Lily and Fred for waking him with their noise. But she saw in the dim light from the living-room that he had another reason for his complaints. Picking up the cot blankets from the floor she tucked him in again and flung open the boxroom door full of righteous indignation.

'If you two think it's funny to pull all the bedclothes off poor dear little Edward,' she said, playing the scene for pathos, 'well, I think it's rotten!'

There was a moment of astonished silence before the protests began, but Beatie was not fooled by the way each one swore that they had not moved from the bed.

'Now who's lying, Lily Gordon?' she said. 'Fred's

only little, but you're old enough to know better,' and as Lily protested again, she drowned her words with the taunting cry of 'Liar, liar, liar!' which Lily had so often used to her.

She closed the boxroom door and set a trap. Fetching the fire-tongs from the living-room, she arranged them quietly where Fred or Lily would fall headlong over them if they came through the doorway. Then she climbed into her parents' bed and lay there silently in the dark. If they tried it again, she thought grimly, she would catch them in the act.

A long time passed before the baby cried again. Beatie sat up quickly wondering if perhaps she had dozed a little. She struck a match and lit a candle in the holder on her bedside table. Poor Edward was kicking his bare legs; his nightdress had worked its way up around his fat tummy, and all the bedclothes were on the floor. Raising the candle and peering towards the boxroom door, she saw that it was closed and the fire-tongs still in place.

She thought hard as she covered Edward up again. Perhaps the baby had kicked the blankets off himself? Her commonsense told her it was not possible: he was too small, the sides of the cot were too high, and the blankets were too far away. So she must have slept and Lily and Fred had been very quiet and cunning . . . But she was not beaten yet. She searched in the jar on the mantelpiece for the key to the boxroom door and locked it. Jess had taken the key away after the three children had persistently locked each other in, causing more noise and shouting and banging than her patience could endure. Now they were all forbidden to take the key from the jar. But Beatie did not care. Ma would understand, she told herself, when she heard how those two horrors had tormented poor Edward. Triumphantly she turned her back on the locked door and then her heart stopped . . . the cot blankets were on the floor again.

Beatie lifted the candle higher, unable to believe what her eyes told her, and saw that there was someone else in the room.

Just at the edge of the circle of light, she could see a little boy with golden hair and a small bright face. He was holding on to the edge of the cast-iron mantelpiece, swinging his feet and laughing up at her. Beatie let out a piercing shriek and dropped the candle. The light went out, the baby cried, Lily and Fred started banging on the boxroom door, and just at that moment of darkest pandemonium, her mother came home after a hard night at the cinema.

We can hardly blame Jess if she was in no mood to listen to explanations. She walloped all three children, with an extra wallop for Beatie for taking the key from the jar. Then she fell into bed with her hands over her ears ignoring both the pained and indignant snuffling from the boxroom and the wailing from the cot.

Before leaving for work on the following day, she threatened the direst consequences if any such thing happened again. Beatie had tried once or twice to tell her strange story but it sounded pretty feeble. The blankets on the floor was a trick of Fred and Lily's, said her mother, and she had dreamed up the little boy. Beatie knew in her heart that it was not so, but how could she convince Jess who had more than enough worries of her own, and who was besieged at the same time by Lily and Fred indignantly telling their version of the night's events. Watching her mother under the barrage of conflicting stories, Beatie suddenly could not bear to see her tired confusion.

'It's all right,' she said quickly. 'Shut up, Lily. Shut up, Fred.' To her surprise, they did, taken aback by a new authority in her voice. And to Jess she said, 'Don't worry, Ma: I'll look after everything until you get back. It will all be peace and quiet, I swear!'

Jess gave her a hug which amply repaid her for the

rash promise, and set out into the night. When she had gone, Beatie wondered what she had let herself in for. She read Fred two chapters of *Stirring Tales of the Empire*, a book which bored her to yawning, in return for his promise of good behaviour. To Lily she read *Favourite Fairy Tales* which Lily loved, having a deep inner conviction that she was herself the victim of a magic spell who would one day be reclaimed by royal parents.

But the moment came at last when the other three were in their beds and Beatie was left to face the unknown. She no longer believed that Lily and Fred had been party to the mischief but she had to be sure. She dared not lock the boxroom door again, but she pulled a large chair in front of it and arranged the fire-tongs so that they would clatter with the slightest movement. Then she climbed into her parents' bed enjoying, even in her anxiety, the spaciousness and the absence of Lily's sharp little toes 'accidentally' digging her in the back.

She left the bedside candle burning but it was low and sputtering. The small flame threw such strange shadows that she almost thought the darkness would be less frightening. It's only a little boy, she told herself firmly, a bit like Fred. I can deal with little boys: he won't get the better of me. She closed her eyes to keep out the moving shadows.

It was as if by even thinking the words, she had laid down a challenge, for at once Edward wailed and she had to get out of bed to pick up the blankets from the floor. She felt more irritated than frightened. 'He's only a baby,' she said crossly to the empty air, and added with a sudden rush of bravado, 'Why don't you pick on someone your own size?'

Having said it she panicked, jumped back into bed and hauled the bedclothes up comfortingly around her chin. She thought she heard the faintest sound of laughter.

'Lily, Fred!' she called. 'Stop that and go to sleep.'

But no answer came from beyond the barricaded door.

Then the candle flickered and almost went out. She saw that the pool of wax was about to overwhelm the flame and she reached to tip a little away into the holder. But her hands were unsteady and she only succeeded in quenching the fragile flame. In the sudden darkness the laughter came again. Beatie reached out a trembling hand to find the matches and as she did so felt a slight but unmistakable movement of her bedclothes. She clutched at them and the slight movement became a strong pull. Something out there in the darkness was trying to take the blankets off her bed . . .

Beatie was seized with a sudden terror of the unknown. She clung to the bedclothes with a wild desperation, feeling that without them she would be defenceless against whatever it was that now seemed to fill the darkness around her. She tried to scream but her throat was impossibly dry and no sound came.

And yet, even at the moment of her greatest fear, there was a streak of pigheadedness in Beatie that would not give in. As the pull grew steadily stronger she gritted her teeth, set her mouth in that stubborn line that so often appeared in the old photographs, and held on. The pull slackened for a moment and quick to take advantage Beatie sat up, gathered an armful of clothes and pinned them to her with arms and elbows as well as fists.

Then the tugging began again almost playful at first then stronger and stronger until the force was moving her whole body, dragging her across the bottom sheet towards the end of the bed. With a strength born of desperation, Beatie took a deep breath, threw herself suddenly backward, and tore the bedclothes from the invisible grasp. She lay back against the pillows breathless and strangely triumphant and for a long time nothing happened. It's gone, she thought, I've beaten it . . . and she felt the same deep sense of satisfaction which filled her when she scored one of her rare victories over Lily and Fred. And that made her do a foolish thing. Relaxing against the pillows, her hold on the bedclothes slack and careless, she poked out her tongue at whatever it was that sulked, defeated, out there in the blackness.

What happened next she had not expected and could never explain. It was as if a whirlwind struck out of nowhere. All the bedclothes went swirling upward out of her grasp, the candle holder flew across the room and the fire-tongs fell with an awful crash from the chair where she had balanced them. Frightened half out of her wits, Beatie threw herself face down on the bed and pulled the pillows over her head to shut out the unearthly clamour.

When she emerged several minutes later, after the pounding of her heart had slackened, everything was quiet. It was odd, she thought, that Eddie was not wailing and there was no sound from Lily or Fred. Though she did not know why, she felt sure that it was all over and the fear went out of her. She found the candlestick on the floor and the matches under the bed and coaxed the candle into a light. Edward was fast asleep, his blankets tucked firmly in place. The chair was still in front of the boxroom door.

Beatie gathered up the scattered bedclothes and re-made her parents' bed. She had promised her mother peace and quiet when she returned and that was what she would find. She put the fire-tongs back in the living-room, restored the chair to its proper place and, making her way into the boxroom, climbed in beside Lily and Fred. They were both sleeping so soundly that even when she pushed them over to make room for herself, they only muttered sleepily and gave way.

'Did it ever happen again?' I asked when Beatie, my mother, now grown as old as Jess, told me this story when I was a girl.

'No,' she said, 'we moved a week later. Ma met a girl at the cinema whose aunt had a much nicer flat to let and was prepared to keep an eye on us during the evening. "Just in case anything should go wrong when I'm out," Ma said.'

'Did you tell her about that night?' I asked.

My mother smiled. 'She wouldn't have believed me, or if she had, she would only have worried.'

'Did you ever find out who the little boy was?'

'Yes, oddly enough, but only by chance. Years later when things were better and Ma had given up her job, young Edward took to sleep-walking for a while. Ma insisted that the front door be locked and chained every evening. 'We don't want him wandering out into the night like that other poor mite," she said. "Which other poor mite?" asked Lily. "At a house where we once lived," said Ma. "It was years ago: you won't remember." But of course *I* did. "Where the old man lived," I told her, "the one with the limp." "Yes," said Ma, surprised. "He told me he once had a little boy who walked in his sleep. One night the child went down the stairs and out into the street and was killed by a passing hansom cab. Such a lovely child too, the old man said, all golden curls and a beautiful smile."'

And a wicked sense of humour, thought Beatie. But she kept her thoughts to herself.

Video Nasty

by

Philip Pullman

It was a cold grey afternoon in November, and the three boys had been hanging around the shopping precinct since mid-morning. They'd had some chips at midday, and Kevin had nicked a couple of Mars bars from the newsagent's, so they weren't hungry. And until they were thrown out of Woolworth's they weren't cold either; but by half-past three they were cold and fed up, and almost wished they'd gone to school.

'How much longer we got to wait?' said David, the youngest boy, to Martin, the oldest.

Martin was fourteen, thin and dark and sharper than the other two by a long way. He looked at his watch. 'Oh, come on,' he said. 'Let's go and see if it's ready.'

He hunched himself inside his anorak and led the way out of the precinct and down one of the old streets that led towards the canal. The cold wind blew crisp packets and old newspapers around their ankles. The boys turned around two corners and stopped outside a little newsagent's, where one of the windows was filled with a display of video cassettes.

'See if there's anyone in there, Kev,' said Martin.

Kevin opened the door, which jangled loudly. The street was empty, apart from an abandoned Datsun without any wheels that stood in a scatter of broken glass half on and half off the pavement. After a few seconds Kevin came out and said, ''S okay.'

The other two went in. The place smelled like all newsagents – a bit chocolatey, a bit smokey, a bit like old comics. There was nothing unusual about it, but David felt his stomach lightening. He pretended to be unconcerned and picked up a paperback that said AQUARIUS: Your Horoscope For 1994. He didn't know if he was Aquarius or what, but he had to look cool.

An old man had come out from the back. He was carrying a mug of tea, and sipped at it before he spoke.

'Yes, lads?' he said.

Martin went up to the counter. 'You got that video in yet?' he said. 'The one you told me about last week?'

The old man took another sip, and narrowed his eyes.

'What one's that? I don't remember you.'

'You said it'd be in today. *Snuff Park*. You told me about it.'

Recognition came into the old man's eyes, and he smiled carefully.

'Course I remember,' he said. 'You got to be careful, that's all. Wait there.'

He put his mug on a shelf and shuffled out. Kevin's frowning, short-sighted eyes flickered to the sweets, but Martin put his hand on his arm, and shook his head. No-one spoke.

After a minute the old man came back with a video cassette, which he put in a brown paper bag. Martin passed over the money; David put back his book and opened the jangling door.

'Bye, lads,' said the old man. 'Enjoy the film.'

'Let's have a look,' said Kevin, once they were outside.

Martin took out the cassette, but there was no picture. There was just a plain white label with 'SNUFF PARK. 112 mins' typed in the centre.

'What's mins?' said Kevin.

'Minutes, you berk. That's how long it lasts,' said Martin, putting it back. 'Come on, let's get a cup of tea. I'm perished.'

'Can't we go to your place?'

'Not yet. I told you. They ain't going out till six. We got to hang about till then.'

As they walked past the abandoned Datsun, one of the doors creaked open. David jumped back out of the way. A thin boy of about his age, wearing torn jeans and trainers and a dirty anorak, was sitting in the driver's seat, with his feet on the pavement. He said something quietly and Martin stopped.

'What?' he said.

'What cassette you got?' said the boy. His voice sounded like the sound your feet make in dry leaves.

'What you want to know for?' said Martin.

The boy shrugged. David thought he could smell him: sharp and dirty and somehow cold. Kevin had his hand on the car door.

'*Snuff Park*,' said Martin after a moment. 'You seen it?'

The boy shrugged again, and said 'Yeah'. He wasn't looking at any of them, but down at the pavement. He scuffed the broken glass with one foot.

No-one else spoke, so Martin turned and walked off. The other two followed. David looked back at the boy in the car, but he hadn't moved. Just before they turned the corner, he shut the car door.

★   ★   ★

In the cafeteria, Martin paid for three cups of tea and brought them to the table by the window where Kevin and David had found a place. David didn't know where Martin got his money from; he assumed Martin's parents gave it to him. He always seemed to have plenty, but he never boasted about stealing it, as Kevin would have done.

He stirred sugar into his tea and watched his reflection in the glass. It was nearly dark outside already.

'What's it about, *Snuff Park*?' said Kevin. 'Sounds crummy.'

'Well it ain't,' said Martin. 'It's a real snuff movie.'

'What's one of them?'

Martin sighed. 'Tell him, Dave,' he said.

David felt a glow of pride at being called Dave.

'It's where they kill someone,' he said. 'Ain't it, Martin?'

Martin nodded and sipped the hot tea.

'What d'you mean?' said Kevin. 'I seen plenty of them.'

'No you ain't,' said Martin. 'They stopped 'em years back. You can't get 'em no more. 'Cept if you know how.'

'I seen all sorts,' said Kevin. 'I seen *Forest of Blood* and *Sawmill*. You seen *Sawmill*?'

'That ain't a snuff movie. You're a berk, you are. This is real. There's someone really killed on this. You see it being done. You ain't never seen that.'

David again felt his stomach lift. He hoped desperately that he wouldn't be sick in front of Martin when the time came. Even thinking about it . . .

'There's that kid again,' said Kevin.

He pointed to the brightly-lit doorway of an electricity board showroom opposite. Sandwich-makers, microwave ovens, cookers, heaters, freezers, and in the doorway gazing in, the thin huddled figure from the car. As they looked he wandered away from there and stared through the window of the supermarket next door.

Martin looked away.

'If you're scared, you needn't watch it,' he said.

'Course I ain't scared,' said Kevin. 'I seen *Sawmill* and I weren't scared of that.'

'This is different,' said Martin.

David looked out of the window again, but the other boy had gone.

*   *   *

Martin turned the key and opened the door. The house was full of darkness and the smell of chips and tobacco smoke. David felt the warmth on his cheeks. He'd never been to Martin's house before, and he looked around curiously as Martin put the hall light on. There was a really smart carpet, and a mirror with all gold round it, and a TV phone. He felt reassured. It was so nice that you couldn't imagine anything horrible happening there. *Snuff Park* might not be all that bad. And he could always close his eyes.

'You going to put it on then?' said Kevin. 'Where's the telly?'

'No hurry. I want something to eat first. Ain't you hungry?'

'What you got to eat?'

'Dunno. Fish and chips'll do. You better eat it now 'cause you won't want to after, will he, Dave?'

'No,' said David. 'Not after.'

'Here,' said Martin to David, handing him a ten-pound note. 'Go round the chippy. Cod and chips three times, all right?'

'Ta, Martin,' said David, and added 'Don't start it without me.'

The chip shop was just around the corner. On his way back, with the soft hot bundles clutched to his chest, David suddenly stopped. The boy from the car was standing outside Martin's front door.

'What do you want?' said David, before he could stop himself.

'You going to watch the video?' said the boy.

David could hardly hear what he said. He supposed the boy had got a cold, or asthma, like David's sister.

'Yeah,' he said.

'Can I watch it?'

'I dunno. It ain't mine, it's my mate's.'

The two boys stood still, not looking at each other.

'I'll ask him,' said David finally, and rang the bell.

When Martin opened the door David said 'I got 'em. Three cod and chips. And this kid was there outside the house. He says he wants to watch the video.'

Martin twisted his mouth. Kevin, behind him, said, 'He'll never take it. He'll never take the pressure.'

'All right, let's see if he does,' said Martin. 'Let him in, then.'

The strange boy came in after David and stood in the living-room while they ate their fish and chips. David offered him some, but he just said, 'No, I don't want none.' After a minute or two he sat down. The others didn't say anything, but ate quickly, and dropped their papers in the fireplace. David could smell the strange boy again. The room was hot, and he dropped his anorak on the thick red carpet, but the strange boy kept his on, and sat with his hands in his pockets, unmoving.

'All right then?' said Martin. 'I'll put it on.'

He fitted the cassette into the machine and sprawled back in a big leather armchair with the remote control. David and Kevin were sitting on the settee, and the other boy was on a dining chair by the table. Martin turned the TV on.

'Smart telly,' said Kevin.

It was a 48-inch. The big screen lifted itself out of the console and filled with colour.

'You seen a snuff picture before?' said Martin to the strange boy.

'Yeah. I seen this one.' They had to strain to hear him.

'This one?' It was plain that Martin didn't believe him. 'You know what happens?'

'Yeah. I seen it hundreds of times.'

'Hundreds? Get lost.'

'Here,' said Kevin. 'Let's watch it with the light out.'

'Stay there,' said Martin. 'Watch this.'

He pressed a button on the remote control, and the big centre light above them faded into darkness. Now the only light came from the screen.

'Smart!' said Kevin.

They found themselves watching a suburban street from the windscreen of a moving car. It was a sunny

70

day. There were lots of trees covered in leaves, and the houses looked nice and big, with lots of space between them.

Then the commentary began.

'*Just an ordinary road in an ordinary English town,*' said a man's voice. It was a strong deep voice, warm and concerned. '*An ordinary summer's day. But for one woman nothing will be the same again. There will never be another summer's day for her.*'

David looked at the strange boy. His eyes were wide and fixed intently on the screen, and his lips were moving unconsciously with the words. David felt queer. He knew now very strongly that he didn't want to watch the film at all. He let his eyes go back to the screen, but tried to make them out of focus so that he couldn't see clearly.

A few minutes passed. There was no more commentary from the film, but suddenly the strange boy said something.

'What?' said Martin.

'I says it's a nice house, ain't it?' said the boy.

Kevin, frowning concentratedly, took no notice. Martin grunted, but David looked at the boy again. Anything to get his eyes off the screen; but nothing had happened yet.

'Must be nice living there,' said the boy, still staring. But his expression was strange; David couldn't understand it.

'Yeah,' he said to the boy.

There was a woman on the screen. She was doing normal things, like washing up and ironing. She was talking to the camera about housework or something. David felt full of fear, almost ready to be sick, because it was all so ordinary, and you knew she was real, and you knew it had really happened, like this, and you knew you were going to see her murdered.

'This is boring,' said Kevin. 'What's she on about?'

'Shut up,' said Martin. 'They got the camera in there to get her confidence.'

'But there ain't nothing happening,' said Kevin. 'She's just bloody talking.'

'She's pretty, ain't she?' said the boy.

The other two fell silent, and turned to him for a moment. Even David sensed it was an odd thing to say.

'Eh?' said Martin.

'I says she's pretty, ain't she. She's really nice.'

'What d'you mean?' said Kevin.

'She's my mum,' said the boy.

There was another silence then. Everything had suddenly changed, and David felt it, but didn't know how or why.

'Eh?' said Martin.

'I says she's my mum. She loves me and I love her.'

The boys shifted in their seats. The pictures on the screen had changed. It was night-time, and the camera was outside the house looking in through the kitchen window. The room was warmly lit; the woman was moving about, alone, watering some big green plants. She bent down and picked up a little baby from what must have been a carry-cot, and cuddled it. But none of the three boys were taking this in: they were paralysed by what the strange boy had said. No-one said that sort of thing.

'He's mad,' said Kevin uneasily.

'Hey, what's your name?' said Martin.

There was no reply. Instead the commentary began again:

'Alone. There is no-one to help. Little does she know that an unseen hand has cut the phone wire. And now . . . the fear begins.'

The boy was mouthing the words as if he knew them by heart. Suddenly from the darkness a stone shattered the kitchen window, and the woman gasped and turned wildly, clutching the baby to her. Her wide-eyed face stared out at them, and then they all saw at once that she *was* his mother.

She was bending now, putting the baby down swiftly. And then another window shattered, and she jumped and cried out.

David's heart was beating like a captured bird.

'Martin –' he started to say, but Martin himself spoke at the same time, loudly, sitting up tensely in his chair and turning to the strange boy.

'What d'you want?' he cried. 'What you come here for?'

Kevin was shifting himself next to David, making himself look small and inconspicuous, like he did in class. Martin's face was twisted and full of hate.

'Just wanted to see –' began the strange boy, but his dry rustling voice was drowned by a scream from the TV. David flicked a sideways look at the screen: a man with a stocking mask had burst into the kitchen. There was a blur in the sound, as if two pieces of film had been joined carelessly, and then the camera was suddenly inside the kitchen with them.

'Martin!' cried David.

'What's the matter?' shouted Martin. He was shaking, glaring at the screen, staring wildly, gripping the remote control. 'You scared? You seen enough?' He pressed the volume switch, and terrible sounds flooded the room. David put his hands over his ears. Kevin was still watching, but he'd curled up very small, and he was holding his fists in front of his mouth.

And the strange boy was still gazing at the screen. The woman was speaking, gabbling desperately, and the boy's eyes followed her and his lips moved with her words.

'Shut up!' Martin yelled. 'Shut up!'

He jumped up and dropped the remote control. The picture faded at once, and the last thing David saw was Martin's face, wet with sweat.

They were in darkness.

No-one moved.

David heard Martin gulping and breathing heavily. He felt sick with fear and shame.

The strange boy said, 'It ain't finished.'

'Shut up!' said Martin fiercely. 'Get out!'

'I can't till it's finished. I always see the end.'

'What you want to watch it for?'

'I always watch it. That's the only time I see her. I like seeing my mum.'

In the darkness his voice sounded more than ever distant, and cold, and strange. David's skin was crawling. Everything was horrible. It had been horrible all day, but this was worse than anything. He thought of his own mum, and nearly sobbed out loud, but stifled it just in time.

'And the baby.' The strange boy spoke again. 'It's a nice baby, ain't it? It looks nice. It must be nice being picked up like that, like what she does. I wish I could remember.'

'What d'you mean?' said Martin hoarsely.

The boy's voice was even quieter now: hardly more than dead leaves falling.

'They killed her and then they set fire to the house. It all burnt up, the baby and all. That was me, that was, that baby. I burnt up all with my mum. But I didn't stop growing up, getting older, like. It must be the video. Sort of kept me going. I seen it hundreds of times. The best bit is where she picks me up. I reckon she must have loved me a lot. That's all I do, watch that video. There ain't nothing else . . .'

He stopped.

Martin stumbled to the door and felt for the light-switch. The room sprang into being around them, all solid and bright, but there was no-one else there. Only a sharp, distant smell remained, and that dwindled after a moment and then vanished completely as if it had never existed. The boy was gone.

74

Dolling Halt

by

Pamela Oldfield

Anna looked up as the carriage door opened. A man entered and closed the door behind him. He was not very tall and he had the palest blue eyes Anna had ever seen. She smiled at him politely then looked away, not wishing to stare. The man did not return her smile but crossed to the window and stared up and down the opposite platform. He then sat down, ignoring Anna completely, and patted his right-hand pocket which bulged slightly. The left-hand pocket contained a folded newspaper. He muttered something in an agitated way.

'I'm sorry,' said Anna, thinking he was addressing her. 'I didn't catch what you said.'

The man gave her a sharp glance without answering and leaped up again to stare anxiously out on to the platform. He took a large watch from his pocket and looked at it impatiently as though eager to be on the way. At that moment the whistle blew and there was a noisy slamming of doors as the train prepared to move out of the station. Anna, from the window seat, watched the station slide past as the train gathered speed.

She was on her way from London to spend a long weekend in the country with her cousin Sarah. Anna was nearly fourteen, a sturdy girl with short brown curls and too many freckles for her own peace of mind. She was what her mother called a 'no nonsense' sort of girl and, except when she was at school, she dressed casually in jeans and a tee shirt. Today she also carried a lightweight anorak and a duffel bag but she had already put these in the overhead rack out of the way.

The man opposite pulled the newspaper from his pocket and began to read. At least, thought Anna, he was pretending to read it. In fact his eyes strayed repeatedly to the door. He lowered the paper suddenly and caught Anna looking at him.

'What did you say?' he snapped.

'I didn't say anything,' she replied, taken aback by his brusque manner. He muttered something inaudible and glanced once more towards the door as though, even at this late stage, he expected it to open and admit someone. At the next station he hid himself behind his paper, but when they moved on again he allowed it to rest in his lap. That gave Anna the chance to study him more closely, and she noticed for the first time the unusual cut of his clothes.

His double-breasted jacket buttoned with four buttons instead of three and there was a high stiff collar to his white shirt. His trousers of matching grey serge had turn-ups, and he wore a flat grey cap. Anna thought it was almost a uniform. She noticed too his large moustache which reminded her of her great grandfather.

The train continued, and after several more stops he seemed to relax a little and he folded up the paper and jammed it back into his pocket. Anna wondered idly what it was he carried in the other pocket. Time passed and she decided it was ridiculous to sit in stony silence.

'My name's Anna,' she told him. 'Anna Court.'

'Oh yes.'

It wasn't a very encouraging remark and he accompanied it with a suspicious glare. Anna began to wonder if she really wanted to share a carriage with such an unfriendly person. She had just decided to find another seat when they next stopped, when the train slowed down and they had reached Bromley. A woman immediately climbed into the carriage.

As soon as she settled herself in her seat she smiled cheerfully at them both.

'Lovely weather we're having,' she began. 'I said to my husband, I'm not going to need a coat but he insisted that I bring it. If this fine weather goes on we shall have nothing to complain about, that's for sure, although of course it could change. That's the thing about the weather in this country, you never know where you are. My husband likes it that way. You wouldn't catch him on the Costa Brava. Sunshine every day, so they say. He likes a bit of variety.'

The woman talked incessantly, and Anna thought ruefully that one of her fellow passengers wouldn't talk and the other one wouldn't stop! Out of the two she preferred the former, for the woman's chatter was uninteresting to say the least. The man retired once more behind his newspaper. Fortunately for Anna's sanity, the woman got out and her place was taken by an elderly nun who was soon immersed in a book.

Anna glanced at her watch. Not much longer and she would be greeting Sarah. The two girls were very close in age and had always been very good friends. At last the train began to slow down, and to Anna's surprise she saw that it had stopped at Dolling Halt. The tiny station, which consisted only of a small wooden platform and a waiting-room, had been closed for as long as Anna could remember and wore an air of prolonged neglect. Grass grew between the wooden planking and the old iron seat was rusty. Wild flowers sprouted around the gate leading to the pathway which was now entirely overgrown. Anna had always found the little station a mournful place and today was no exception.

The train whistled once and then all was still. The nun had apparently dozed off and Anna suddenly realised how warm and humid the air had become. The man was eyeing Anna with a strange expression on his face, but neither of them spoke. Anna would be getting out at the next stop and she wished the train would resume its journey. Only two more miles, she reflected, and then she and Sarah would be exchanging their news and making plans for the next few days, and this rather unsatisfactory journey would be over. After a few moments' silence Anna began to wonder about the reason for the delay and put her head out of the window to see what was happening outside. A cow on the line, perhaps, she thought. There was nothing to be seen, and a strange stillness seemed to have taken possession of the train and the surrounding landscape. There were no sounds, not even bird song, she noticed with growing uneasiness.

Then, with a suddenness that made her jump, the man pushed her out of the way, opened the door and sprang down on to the deserted platform. To her intense amazement he began to run wildly up and down the platform, lashing out in all directions with his arms, as though fighting off invisible assailants. He tried to get out of the gate but suddenly staggered backwards and fell heavily to the ground. He doubled up, groaning loudly, covering his head with his arms as though to protect himself.

Anna was horrified. 'Is he having a fit of some kind?' she cried. 'Oh poor man.'

She glanced at the nun but the old woman slept on. Anna shook her by the arm.

'That man,' she cried. 'He's in some kind of trouble. He may be ill. We must help him.'

To her surprise the nun remained fast asleep. She shook her more roughly but without success. Anna stared at her in disbelief. 'What on earth is happening?' she whispered with growing apprehension. She ran back to the door of the carriage and looked out. The man lay on the ground with a look of abject terror on his face. His cap lay in the grass at the edge of the platform. Incredibly no-one had gone to his assistance. Anna jumped down on to the platform and was at once struck by the intense humidity of the air. As she looked along the train it seemed to her as though it slumbered in the sunshine, made slightly unreal by the shimmering effect of the light.

'Almost like a mirage!' she whispered.

With an effort she willed herself to approach the fallen man who was now struggling to his feet.

'Get away from me, all of you!' he shouted hoarsely. 'Get back or you'll be sorry. I mean it. Stay away from me.'

The prickle of unease that Anna had so far experienced was magnified into fear as he pulled a pistol from his pocket and waved it around him.

'One of you is going to get this,' he shouted wildly. 'Who's it going to be, eh? The first man who tries to take me is going to die.' Now Anna was quite sure the man was out of his mind. He might even be hallucinating. She did not understand such things but she did know that she was the only person on the platform. Where on earth was everyone else? Why did no-one come to help her? Glancing back towards the train she saw no faces at the windows, and the unnatural quiet persisted. It was as though there was no-one in the world except herself and the madman.

The man cried out again. 'You won't take me alive.'

He turned to Anna, and she was appalled by the crazed look in his pale blue eyes.

'Don't shoot,' she begged shakily. 'I'm not going to hurt you. No-one is.'

He only shook his head wonderingly.

Around them the inexplicable stillness was like a veil, shutting the two of them off from reality.

'I only want to help you,' Anna began, but suddenly he thrust out his foot as though to kick someone and then he fired into the air. Terrified, Anna backed away from him. She no longer felt able to cope with the situation, which was becoming dangerous, and she was angry that no-one else was prepared to leave the train and help her.

'For heaven's sake!' she shouted. 'Won't someone help me? Please!'

Silence greeted her words.

She screamed at the top of her voice. 'Somebody. Anybody. Please help.'

Still the awful quiet prevailed.

Then without warning the man made a dash for the waiting-room and hurled himself against the door. It burst open and he went headlong through the doorway and out of sight.

Nothing happened for a moment or two and then a single shot rang out.

'Oh no,' whispered Anna.

Alone on the desolate platform Anna froze. Had he killed himself? Panic-stricken she ran to the nearest carriage and wrenched open the door. Inside a man and two boys lolled in their seats, their eyes closed. In the next compartment two women dozed. It was the same in the next carriage.

'They're all asleep!' whispered Anna incredulously. 'But how can that be?'

After a further hesitation she reluctantly approached the waiting-room and glanced inside. The man lay slumped against the far wall, motionless, the pistol still in his right hand. Timidly she went inside and knelt beside him. There was a small wound in his temple and blood trickled down his face and stained his collar.

'He's dead!' she whispered, horrified.

For what seemed an eternity she could not think sensibly, but then her wits returned. Someone must fetch an ambulance and inform the police. With a flash of inspiration she thought of the engine driver. He would hardly be dozing and he would surely be responsible for the safety of his passengers. The driver must be awake and alert even if nobody else was.

As if to prove this point the train gave a sudden lurch and began to move. Anna gave a cry of terror. The train was leaving and she would be left alone with the tragedy. She ran outside.

'Stop!' she shouted. 'Something has happened. You must stop. I tell you there's been an accident – a shooting.'

To her dismay the train continued to gather speed. As it passed her she saw faces at the window as people regarded her curiously. Anna felt as though she was taking part in a nightmare. She beat her fists on the train as it rolled past and then, despairing, let her arms fall to her side. She watched the train as it went round the bend in the track and disappeared.

Suddenly the oppressive heat lifted and the birds began to sing. Anna shook her head in bewilderment. Something very strange was taking place and she was helpless to do anything about it. Fearfully she went back into the waiting-room and there another, even greater, shock awaited her. It was empty!

Anna gasped, unable to believe her eyes.

'He must be here,' she muttered. 'Two minutes ago he was here. I know he was. This is impossible.'

She did not know whether to be pleased or sorry that the body had gone. If it had been here, then where was it now? But if it had never existed – Perhaps it was *she* that was mad. Perhaps she had imagined it all. But that was impossible, for why should she have got out of the train in the first place?

Slowly she searched every inch of the tiny platform but there was no sign of the man and his cap was no longer lying in the grass. When she had satisfied herself that there was no body and therefore no reason to fetch an ambulance or call the police, Anna began to walk along the side of the track in the direction of the next station. She was thankful it was only two miles.

On the way she remembered that her duffel bag and

anorak were on the train. She would have to report it when she reached the station. She wondered if Sarah was still waiting for her. She would think she had missed the train, thought Anna, and hopefully would wait to meet the next one. One thing was certain. Nobody was going to believe her story.

*　　*　　*

Sarah *was* still waiting and the two girls hugged each other delightedly. After Anna had reported her missing belongings they walked back along the lane together and Anna told Sarah what had happened. To her relief her cousin listened in rapt silence.

'And I *know* I didn't imagine it all,' Anna assured her. 'It was real. All of it. He was as real as you are. For goodness' sake, Sarah, tell me I'm not crazy.'

Sarah shook her head. 'You're not crazy,' she told her, 'but you did not see someone as real as I am. What you saw was the ghost of Jack Mills. No, don't ask me what I mean. I can show you something when we get home that will explain it better than I can.'

At home Anna greeted her aunt and then the two girls hurried upstairs to Sarah's bedroom where she immediately rummaged in an old chest and brought out a scrap book.

'We found this in the attic when we moved in,' she told Anna. 'It belonged to the previous owner and it's full of old postcards and newspaper cuttings.' She began to turn the pages. 'Ah, here it is. Listen to this.' She began to read and Anna listened spellbound. It was the account of a murder in London. A chauffeur had shot his employer and had attempted to escape by train. The police had joined the train further along the line and the final battle had been fought out at Dolling Halt, where the murderer made a last bid for freedom. 'So you see,' Sarah explained. 'When he realised he would never escape he shot himself, and his ghost has haunted the station ever since. That's why they had to close it down.

No-one would wait on the platform after dark. They were too scared.'

'So I saw the whole drama being acted out again!' gasped Anna. 'But why me? Why today?'

Sarah pointed to the date of the old cutting. 'Today's date,' she said quietly.

'But why –?' Anna began, but then she stopped. Sarah could not explain that intense, shimmering heat or the silence. No-one could tell her how a whole train and its passengers could slumber so soundly while a tragedy from the past was re-enacted around them. Perhaps, Anna thought wisely, some things are beyond comprehension and better that way.

Nathan's True Self

by

Alison Prince

Mr Martin, masterful in a pale blue sweater with the sleeves pushed up, waved his script at the would-be cast assembled in the school hall. 'As I see it,' he said, 'Macbeth got in the kind of mess that could happen to anyone.'

'Martin's a twit,' Edge muttered to Nathan, who grinned, but hoped Edge was not going to be too outrageous. The annual play was the only thing which made school tolerable, and Nathan wanted to be in it.

'He's one of a gang of Scottish toughs all fancying their chances of being the next king,' Mr Martin went on. 'In those days the throne was up for grabs, you see, open to whoever could prove the best claim. It was a damn' silly system really, known as tanistry. Caused no end of quarrelling.'

Edge yawned hugely and Nathan wished Mr Martin would stop trying to be engaging and get on with the auditions.

'In many ways, Macbeth himself was a fall-guy,' continued Mr Martin. 'In real life he was married to a ferocious woman called Gruach. Shakespeare must have thought it was a pretty ghastly name, so he just called her Lady Macbeth. Now, Gruach *was* of royal blood, and she was hell-bent on getting her husband to the throne of Scotland.'

'Did she do it?' asked Kate Lee.

'Oh, yes,' said Mr Martin. 'She was unstoppable. That was the trouble. Macbeth liked the idea of being

King but, left to himself, he'd never have done much about it. He wouldn't have murdered Duncan if his wife hadn't pushed him into it. And that was the fatal mistake. He betrayed his own, true self by trying to meet someone else's standards.'

'Huh!' said Edge.

Knowing what he meant, Nathan commented, 'Schools try to make you meet someone else's standards all the time.' The truth of this struck him more forcefully as he thought about it. Mr Martin was busy defending the educational standpoint, but Nathan stopped listening. What *was* the true self, he wondered? In his own case, it seemed to be the thing that nobody liked.

'*Macbeth* is supposed to be unlucky, isn't it?' asked Kate.

'Yes, it is,' said Mr Martin, happy to change the subject. 'Quoting *Macbeth* in a dressing room, specially on a first night, is supposed to be disastrous. It's a very black, weird sort of play.'

Edge yawned again, more elaborately, and Mr Martin looked at him. 'That's why I've invited all the school villains to be in it,' he said. 'This isn't a play for good boys and girls. I want it to be tough and violent.'

'Oh, give it a rest,' muttered Edge with disillusion.

Mr Martin glanced down at his script then said, 'Gavin Egerton, I'd like you to try for Macduff. He's the one who kills Macbeth in the end, and he's always played as being terribly *good*. I want him to be a rough-neck like the rest of them.'

'You got to be joking,' said Edge. 'I only came in here because it's raining.'

'We'll try people for the Macduff part first,' said Mr Martin firmly. 'Come on, Gavin.'

'I can't read that stuff,' Edge protested. 'All old-fashioned rubbish, innit?'

Mr Martin played his trump card. 'I've re-written the whole thing in common English,' he said. '*Very* common English in some parts. The powers that be are going to be furious. Come on – give it a try.'

Nathan didn't think Edge would do it but, to his surprise, his friend got up and minced towards the steps at the side of the stage in a parody of camp theatricality, smoothing his spiky hair with one hand, the other on his hip. Mr Martin didn't seem to mind.

While the contenders for Macduff were being handed their scripts, general conversation broke out in the hall.

'I think it's a smashing play,' said Kate. 'Specially the witchy bits.'

'They're stupid,' said Tony Green. 'Nobody believes in all that stuff.'

'Yes, they do!' said Kate. 'Look at that woman who goes round saying she can get in touch with the spirits of people's departed loved ones. Her meetings are crammed to the doors. And we play the glass game at home, and *that* works!'

'What's the glass game?' asked Jenny Howlett.

'You put a circle of letters round an upturned glass and everyone rests their fingers on it and asks it questions. And the glass slides from letter to letter, spelling out the answers,' Kate explained.

Nathan stared at her. 'Go on – you push it,' he said.

'No,' said Kate calmly. 'It really works.' Her black eyes looked into his from under the mass of dark hair and Nathan felt a slight shiver. She might almost be a witch herself. 'You must try it,' Kate said. 'Come round one evening. You know where I live, don't you? In the flats over the launderette in Burnham Street.'

Nathan laughed. 'Don't you mean Birnam Wood?' he said. The witches had told Macbeth to fear no man until Birnam came to Dunsinane.

'It's not spelt the same, twit,' said Kate. 'Our flat's number thirty-three.' Several people raised their eyebrows and giggled, and Nathan felt harassed. It was widely said that Kate fancied him.

87

When Nathan's audition for the part of Macbeth was over, he went in search of Edge, who had gone out after giving a raucous account of Macduff's feelings on hearing that his wife and children had been murdered by Macbeth. The rain had stopped and he found Edge sitting on the concrete behind the bicycle sheds. His hands dangled on his knees and a cigarette dangled in his mouth. His eyes were half-shut against the smoke and he did not bother to look round as Nathan sat down beside him. That was the good thing about Edge, Nathan thought. He never expected anything. He seemed as self-contained as a tree or a stone, totally indifferent and undemanding. Sometimes it made Nathan feel very shut out, and he wished he could do something to make Edge approve of him, or even notice him. But it was a waste of time. Edge simply did what he thought he would do.

'Coming out tonight?' asked Edge, squinting at the wire netting which ran along the top of the wall. Rain-drops hung from its rusty strands.

'Yes,' said Nathan without hesitation. His stomach churned with apprehension and delight. 'Where?'

'Down the river,' said Edge. 'Where we had the Renault.'

'Okay,' said Nathan, trying to sound casual. He re-membered the Renault with uneasy joy. By some piece of undreamed-of luck, it had been standing by the rear entrance to one of the gardens belonging to the big houses by the river, its tailgate open as if someone had left it for a moment while they carried something indoors. And its keys were in it. Edge had been in the driver's seat like a flash, and away they went, over Hammersmith Bridge and away through south London, expecting to be stopped by the police at any moment because the gearbox wasn't like anything Edge had driven before and it made some pretty weird noises. Coming back, they'd turned into a dead-end street by mistake and Edge couldn't find reverse, so they'd gone through a gap in the fence and driven across a whole field of allotments until they came to a road on the far side. When they dumped the car back in Chiswick there was a Brussels sprout plant stuck under its bumper.

'Half seven,' said Edge.

'Right,' said Nathan.

*　　*　　*

Most of the houses in the tall Georgian terrace had garages opening on to the riverside street which ran along the rear of their gardens, but a number of cars were parked at the kerbside.

'Volvo, BMW, Audi,' said Edge, surveying them. 'Porsche over there, look. Makes you sick.'

'And there are people who've got nowhere to live,' said Nathan, looking at the gracious houses. Reproduction carriage lamps and stone figures stood among the laburnum trees in the gardens.

'Don't start on your Socialist crap,' said Edge.

'I wasn't,' said Nathan, hurt. He was quite proud of his mother for being a lecturer at the LSE, but sometimes it had its disadvantages. Edge was scouting his way along the row of cars, feeling their door handles hopefully. Foiled, he crouched by the front wheel of a Volvo and Nathan heard the hiss of air as he let the tyre down.

'How d'you do that?' Nathan enquired, going to join Edge. 'Just press the valve thing in?'

'No, that's too slow,' said Edge, and displayed a small tool he held in his hand. 'Just take the valve out. Much more nuisance.'

'Someone'll be late for his posh office tomorrow,' Nathan agreed.

'Keep a look-out,' Edge instructed. He went round to the road side of the car and crouched by its rear wheel. Nathan glanced up and down the street, trying to still the uneasy fluttering in his stomach. As always, he half-wished he wasn't here. But there was something

89

addictive about the fear. When people like Mr Dobson, the Senior Master, started on about Nathan's maths with the sarcasm which hurt despite all defences, there was a kind of security in reflecting that Dobson didn't know the half of it.

Quite suddenly, the door of the nearest garage opened and a woman came out. She was only a few yards from Nathan, and the light which shone from the garage behind her fell full on his face. 'Hello!' she said in a voice which, to Nathan's horror, was full of friendly recognition. He knew afterwards he should have stayed where he was, but his instinct to avoid being seen had already caused him to duck away behind the car. The Volvo sagged a little as the air went out of another tyre, and Edge looked up at Nathan with a grin. He caught the alarm on Nathan's face and immediately jumped to his feet and sprinted away down the street. Nathan followed him. The woman shouted after them, 'I know who you are! You won't get away with this!' Nathan did not look back.

They pelted along the leafy roads until they reached the shop-lined High Street. A bus pulled up at the traffic lights and Edge jumped on to it. Nathan followed him up its stairs to sit on the front seat. 'I haven't got any money,' he said, panting.

'Neither have I,' said Edge. 'Doesn't matter. Long as we're away before the fuzz get there.'

When the Jamaican conductor arrived, Edge said politely, 'Piccadilly, please.'

'Don't muck about,' said the conductor.

Edge looked innocent. 'This bus goes to Piccadilly, doesn't it?' he queried. 'It says so on the front.'

'You goin' the wrong way,' said the conductor. 'As if you didn't know. Twenty pence.'

'Don't be funny,' said Edge. He got up and made his way to the stairs, Nathan following.

'I had you kids before, bumming rides with that old

trick,' said the conductor. 'Just you get off this bus.'

When Edge and Nathan got down at the next stop, a police car flashed past, going the way they had come. 'That woman *did* ring the cops,' said Nathan uneasily.

Edge shrugged. 'They won't be much bothered,' he said. 'Got more to think about.' He didn't even look as if he'd been running, Nathan thought enviously.

'See you,' said Edge abruptly, and swung himself on to another passing bus. Dismissed, Nathan stared after him bleakly. Edge, leaning out negligently from the bus's platform, gave Nathan a rare grin and a warm, leisured thumbs-up sign. Then he was gone.

It was a long walk home. Nathan set out in an odd mixture of contentment and dread. Tomorrow, he knew, he would regret the whole thing and resolve to say no next time Edge asked him. At this moment, though, with his heart still beating fast after the run, he felt charged with life. Most of the time his mind rambled slackly through imaginary events in an effort to shut out the dreary reality of school. The hours he spent with Edge were sharp and real, with no division between the thinking and the doing.

As he walked, the euphoria faded and Nathan began to worry. The woman who came out of the garage had recognised him. There was no doubt of that. She would describe him to the police. She might even know his name. Her face was vaguely familiar to Nathan, but he had no idea where he had seen her. He pondered over the question of what to do. If questioned, the best chance was to deny the whole thing. She couldn't *prove* it was him. But he needed to believe that he had been doing something else. Lies, he had discovered, were difficult to sustain unless he had first convinced himself of their truth. After that, it was just acting. Where could he have been this evening since he left home at seven o'clock?

Musing, Nathan passed a garage and a discount warehouse and came to a row of shops with flats over them.

The last shop in the row was a launderette and, glancing up at the street name above it, he realised that he was in Burnham Street. Kate Lee lived above the launderette. Perhaps she could be persuaded to provided the basis of his fictional activities this evening. After all, she had pestered him long enough.

Nathan walked through the alleyway by the launderette and went up the concrete steps which led to the flats. He knocked on the door of number thirty-three and it was opened by a thin, dark-haired woman. A grey cat lay across her shoulders comfortably, long paws dangling. She seemed unaware of it. 'Yes?' she said.

'Er – could I speak to Kate?' asked Nathan.

The woman turned from the door and shouted, 'Kate!' The cat gave a sudden, yowling mew but did not move from her shoulders. Kate came into the hall and said, 'Nat! Great to see you. Come on in. Mum, this is Nat Prothero. He's come to try the glass game, haven't you, Nat?'

Nathan had forgotten about the glass game but he was glad to accept Kate's explanation for his arrival.

'I'll make some coffee,' said Mrs Lee.

Conversation over the coffee was difficult. Kate's black eyes rested on Nathan with a disturbing intensity and he began to feel that this had been a silly idea. Then Mrs Lee, with the cat still draped across her shoulders, swept the fringed cloth off a circular table and produced a box of small cardboard squares, each one with a black letter printed on it. These she arranged in alphabetical order round the edge of the table, leaving a gap at one side for the word Yes, and at the other for No. Kate took a heavy-bottomed glass tumbler from the cupboard and inverted it in the middle of the table.

Suddenly Nathan had no doubt that the game worked. In his imagination the glass was already sliding, spelling out words as if sensitive to some secret radio signal. He sat down at the table with Kate and her mother and the three of them placed their fingers lightly on the glass. Nathan expected to feel a tingle of electricity, but there was nothing.

'Is there anybody there?' Kate asked the glass in a matter-of-fact way. After a moment it twitched towards Yes, then stopped.

'Come on,' Mrs Lee encouraged it. 'Tell us if you're there.'

The glass slid decisively to Yes then, after a pause, returned to the centre of the table.

'Who are you?' enquired Kate.

Unhesitatingly, the glass slid from letter to letter, spelling out the word, 'M-a-c-b-e-t-h'. Kate looked at Nathan across the table and said, 'You've been thinking about it.'

'I haven't,' he said with truth. 'I've been –' But the evening's events were too complicated to express briefly. 'I've been busy,' he amended.

Kate frowned, scenting mystery. 'Doing what?' she demanded. But, to Nathan's relief, Mrs Lee was asking the glass another question. 'Macbeth, what have you to tell us?'

The glass moved quickly. 'B-e-w-a-r-e,' it spelt out.

Kate laughed. 'The ides of March?' she said. 'Oh, no. Wrong play.'

The glass rotated in a fretful circle in the centre of the table and Mrs Lee frowned at her daughter. 'Don't interrupt, Kate,' she said. 'They never like it.' Politely, she added to the glass, 'Do go on, Macbeth.' The hair on Nathan's scalp began to crawl. This was not a joke.

'E-d-g-e,' the glass spelled.

'The edge of what?' questioned Mrs Lee, but Kate glanced at Nathan, understanding. 'Gavin Egerton, you mean?' she suggested to the glass, and it moved quickly to Yes.

'Who's Gavin Egerton, for Heaven's sake?' asked Mrs Lee rather petulantly, and frowned when Kate said, 'A friend of Nat's.' 'I do hope this isn't going to be a *boring* evening,' she said.

Nathan leaned forward. He had no doubt that the glass was speaking personally to him. 'Why should I beware of Edge?' he asked. His mouth was dry.

The glass was reluctant to move. Then it crept slowly from letter to letter. 'D-e-a-t-h,' it spelled. It returned to the centre and was still. Suddenly the cat leapt from Mrs Lee's shoulder to the table and thence to the floor, scattering letters as it went.

'Oh, *Satan*!' scolded Mrs Lee. '*Naughty* boy!' The cat ran out of the door and Mrs Lee, still retaining contact with the glass, bent down to retrieve the fallen letters. Nathan's face was white. He took his fingers off the glass.

'Don't do that!' cried Kate. 'We might lose the spirit. You're really good at it – we haven't had such exciting messages for ages.'

'I don't need to do any more,' said Nathan. 'I mean – okay, I know it works.'

Kate looked at him, frowning. 'You don't want to take it too seriously,' she said. 'It does work, but we always think it picks up what people are thinking. It must have got Edge from you. Perhaps you're worried about him or something?'

'I must go,' said Nathan, not wanting to answer this question in front of Kate's mother and yet longing to talk to someone who would understand. 'Thanks for the coffee.'

'Welcome,' said Mrs Lee a little absently. 'Did Satan have his supper, Kate? It's funny of him to go off like that.' She got up from the table and went into the kitchen in search of the cat and Kate, too, abandoned the glass and accompanied Nathan to the front door. There, she stared at him through narrowed eyes and said, 'There's something the matter, isn't there?'

'Not really,' said Nathan. 'But – would you mind if

I said I'd been here since half past seven? Just if anyone should ask. But I don't think they will.'

Kate put her head on one side. Her black eyes gleamed with malicious interest. 'What have you been up to?' she asked. 'And why should you think I'll tell lies for you?'

Nathan shrugged, unable to frame any reply. He turned to open the door but she was there quickly, barring his way, face upturned. 'You don't have to worry,' she murmured. 'I *will* tell lies for you.'

Suddenly, with a mixture of excitement and alarm, Nathan realised that she wanted him to kiss her. Until now, his sexual experience had been limited to furtive perusals of *Playboy* and some lurid dreams. He pecked at her tentatively and she clasped him with startling strength, pressing her mouth to his for what seemed an impossibly long time. He wondered if she would think it rude if he went on breathing through his nose. Otherwise, he feared he might burst.

Mrs Lee, coming out of the kitchen with the cat back in its place on her shoulders, looked at Kate and Nathan casually and said, 'Shall I put the glass game away?'

'No,' said Kate. 'I want to have another go. Tell Macbeth to wait, if he's still there.'

Nathan had not realised that unimpeded breathing was such a pleasure, but he was already beginning to want to kiss Kate again. Her black eyes stared up at him. 'Mum will have to lie too,' she said, and for a wild moment Nathan wondered if he was expected to kiss Mrs Lee as well. 'You can leave her to me, though,' said Kate, as if reading his thoughts. Then she added deliberately, 'If you're my steady boy-friend she'll count you as part of the family. She'll stick up for you like anything.'

Nathan nodded uneasily. What had he let himself in for? 'Thanks,' he said.

'Come round tomorrow,' Kate instructed. 'A bit

earlier. About seven. There's a film I'd like to see.'

'I haven't got any money,' Nathan confessed.

Kate smiled. 'But you're a big boy now,' she said, with a trace of menace. 'I'm sure you can find some.' She kissed him again, more briefly, and was gone.

Nathan reeled home in a horrified daze. In his mind, the glass still slid from letter to letter, taking his unresisting fingers with it. Beware of Edge. Beware of death. And beware, he said to himself, oh, beware of Kate Lee.

★ ★ ★

At school the next day, Nathan was summoned to the Headmaster's office.

'I have had a very serious report about you,' said Mr Lombard, staring at Nathan over the top of his spectacles. 'One of our Governors, Mrs Selsdon, saw two boys last night, interfering with her car. She recognised one of them as you.'

Nathan looked shocked. 'No, sir,' he said.

'Mrs Selsdon is in no doubt,' said Mr Lombard gravely. 'She has seen you in several school plays over the years, and she is frequently in the building.'

So that was why her face looked familiar. Nathan shook his head in injured innocence as he waited for the inevitable question. It came.

'Where *were* you last night?' asked Mr Lombard.

Nathan aimed at a mixture of pride and boyish embarrassment. It was not difficult to achieve. 'I went round to see Kate Lee,' he said.

Mr Lombard gave a faint sigh. 'And she will of course testify to that,' he said.

'I expect so,' said Nathan easily as he met the Headmaster's eye. 'I mean, it *is* true.'

Mr Lombard sat back in his chair. 'If it were not for your association with Gavin Egerton, Nathan, I would be inclined to believe you,' he said. 'As it is, I do not. And I can only advise you to get out of this game you are playing while you still can. It's very dangerous.'

Nathan allowed utter bewilderment to spread across his face, but Mr Lombard was not impressed. 'You can go,' he said coldly. As Nathan turned to the door, he added, 'The boy with you was Gavin, I suppose?'

But Nathan had not relaxed his guard. 'When I go to see my girl-friend, sir, I don't take anyone with me,' he said smoothly.

'Get out of here,' said Mr Lombard.

*　　*　　*

Nathan closed the Headmaster's door behind him, more shaken by the interview than he had admitted. He found that he felt oddly tired. It was all a very big effort, being what other people expected him to be, especially as they all wanted something different. His mother assumed that he was talented and capable, and Mr Martin took it for granted that Drama came first. Dobson considered him a hooligan and the rest of the class thought he was a bit of a nutter. And Kate Lee – but Nathan flinched from thinking about Kate Lee. Edge was the only one with the right idea, he thought. He didn't expect anything.

Perhaps, Nathan reflected, life was all acting. Nothing but pretence, day after day, on and on. Tomorrow and tomorrow and tomorrow, as it said in the play, to the last syllable of recorded time.

Nathan scowled as he strode, doom-laden, down the corridor, which was now crowded with people for morning break. He glared at them. All our yesterdays, he thought, have lighted fools the way to dusty death. Good old Bill. Dead himself for centuries now, but still alive in the words which ran like music in the mind. Acting was all right when it didn't get mixed up with real life. It was a world of its own. He hoped Mr Martin had not completely wrecked *Macbeth* by converting it into modern English.

A small group of people were clustered round the Drama notice board. Looking over their shoulders,

Nathan saw that they were looking at the newly-published cast list. It was headed by his own name. Macbeth – Nathan Prothero. He did not wait to look at the rest but walked on, keeping the inward smile which warmed his mind to a mere lift of the eyebrows. It seemed that the crowds parted for him. A vision of the sliding glass and its threatening message came as a disturbing memory, but Nathan dismissed it. 'I bear a charmèd life,' he murmured. The circlet of gold lay light upon his head and he loosened his sword in its scabbard.

Kate Lee, Nathan found to his alarm, had been cast as Lady Macbeth. She approached him in the fifth-year common room, as self-possessed as a cat. 'So I am to be your lady,' she said, slipping her arm through his while her friends giggled. 'Aren't you pleased?'

'I'm shattered,' Nathan said, conscious of the grinning onlookers, who were well aware of Nathan's previous evasion tactics where Kate was concerned.

'Come, my lord,' Kate insisted, making for an un-occupied corner of the room. Nathan paced in step beside her, masking his acceptance of her suggestion in theatricality. He should have known she would get the part of Lady Macbeth. Nobody else could be so ruthless. Or so mad.

As if by common consent, they stopped and looked at each other. Kate said, 'Nat, you've got to stop going around with Edge.'

'Why?' asked Nathan.

Kate's dark eyebrows drew together. 'Mum and I had another go at the glass game last night,' she said, avoiding Nathan's eye. 'And it was still Macbeth, saying you were going to die.' She looked up. 'And you're not, you mustn't. You're going on the stage, and so am I, and we're going to be great.'

The glass kept on sliding. Nathan shook his head helplessly. Kate's expectation for him reached out beyond school, all the way into his foreseeable future. He felt utterly trapped.

Whistles and catcalls were coming from the group he and Kate had left. Kate smiled, unruffled. 'My worthy lord,' she quoted ironically, 'your noble friends do lack you.'

Nathan glared across the room. 'Let them lack,' he said.

There was no escape. No refuge – except Edge. Nathan turned abruptly and went out. Edge might be behind the cycle sheds. And Edge, blessedly, had no views about Nathan. He simply didn't give a damn.

'See you tonight!' Kate called after him, and it was not a question. Nathan pretended he had not heard.

*   *   *

Edge said he had no money and, even if he had, he was not going to lend any to Nathan to take some tart out. 'Find your own,' he said. 'Same as I do.'

Nathan knew how Edge found his money. A purse visible among the shopping in a basket, goods filched from the corner shop and sold to the first-year kids, a hand-out from an illicit street trader for tipping him off when the cops were coming. Somehow, Nathan could not quite cast himself in that rôle. Or, as Edge more simply put it, he hadn't got the bottle.

*   *   *

'M'm,' said Nathan's mother absently, her eyes still following the tidy lines of something a student had written. 'I hope she's not an *expensive* kind of girl.'

Economics, Nathan thought, was an awful subject. It warped people's outlook. 'She lives in a flat over a launderette,' he said.

'It doesn't follow that she's not expensive,' his mother argued, looking up from the script. 'Or that she's not silly,' she added. 'Silly people are such a waste of one's time.'

Nathan turned away and said, 'Oh, forget it.' But

out of the corner of his eye he saw that his mother was fishing in her bag. Running his fingers over the ugly Cretan paperweight on his mother's desk, he hung about, hating himself.

★   ★   ★

'I don't want you going around with Edge,' Kate repeated as they were walking back to her flat from the cinema.

Nathan wanted to tell her to mind her own business. He wished he had not let her worm the whole story out of him, about the evenings spent in sabotage, about the narrow squeaks with the police, and the fear and the exhilaration of it all. 'Edge is all right,' he said.

'Edge is crazy,' said Kate. She turned to face Nathan, stopping in the middle of the pavement. 'Listen, you think he doesn't expect anything of you. But he does. He expects *you* to expect nothing.' In the light of the orange street lamps, her face was putty-white, but the black eyes stared up at him with undimmed intensity. 'Something awful's going to happen,' she said. 'Something to do with Edge. I know it is. You're running out of time, Nat.'

Nathan did not reply. Shakespeare's words ran in his head. Out, out, brief candle. Macbeth, too, he thought, must sometimes have wished that time *would* run out, and release him from the entangling mesh of trouble.

★   ★   ★

As the term continued, things got worse. Kate was temperamental and demanding, expecting Nathan to take her out frequently and throwing fits of jealousy when he did anything on his own, particularly if it involved Edge. And yet her dislike of Edge seemed to be purely personal, for she raised no objections to Nathan's increasing involvement in petty crime. Blackly, Nathan recognised that it gave her more power to threaten him with exposure. She was not averse to spending the money which resulted from his activities, but the unspoken blackmail was always there.

When Nathan had been forced to overcome his scruples in order to 'find', as Edge put it, money to take Kate out, his guilty exploits with Edge had become more risky. He was often terrified, but he knew now that he had achieved equal status with Edge. There was no need to say anything, but the grin which passed between them was enough. And, although Kate menaced him, Nathan found himself increasingly excited by her. Their evenings spent together made the enforced childhood of his days at school seem ludicrous. The only member of staff who did not grumble about him these days was Mr Martin, whose production of *Macbeth* was gaining impetus.

Although Nathan yearned for the rolling sonority of Shakespeare's language, he had to admit that the Martin version was forceful. To his surprise, Edge, cast in the role of Macduff, continued to attend quite a lot of rehearsals, though this was mainly because he enjoyed the sword fight with Nathan at the end of the play. They had practised this until it was fast and accurate.

During one lunchtime rehearsal, Nathan stood in the wings and watched Edge in the scene where he had just discovered the corpse of Duncan. Tony Green as Lennox had just come off and stood beside him. 'Wake up, you lot!' Edge was shouting in Mr Martin's basic words. 'Anyone would think you were dead yourselves, lying in your beds like corpses! You're just playing at it – come in here and see the real thing!' Kate, too, was watching Edge through narrowed eyes as she waited to enter from the other side of the stage.

'She's got it in for Edge,' said Tony. Nathan said nothing and Tony went on. 'Jenny says Kate really fancied Edge. She got him to take her out once or twice last year, but he gave her the brush-off. Didn't want to know. You can understand it. I mean, he's just not the sort. But she hasn't forgotten it.'

Nathan's pent-up stress boiled into anger. 'What are you trying to do?' he demanded. 'Make trouble?'

Tony's round face looked startled. He was as clumsy in mind as he was in body, Nathan thought contemptuously, always falling over things and getting everything wrong. So disgustingly anxious to please.

'No, of course not,' said Tony, distressed. 'I mean – you're not serious about Kate, are you? I thought – well, we can all see she's after you but it just seemed a bit of a joke.'

'Some joke,' said Nathan, tight-faced.

'Sorry,' said Tony. 'Didn't mean –'

'Oh, forget it,' said Nathan. He felt years older than Tony.

$$\star \quad \star \quad \star$$

Edge had never been very consistent about attending school, but in the last, frantic week before the school play he was away altogether. Mr Martin looked depressed and said Tony Green had better stand by to do Macduff and the Second Murderer could be Lennox. 'Then who's going to be the Murderer?' asked Jenny Howlett. Mr Martin shrugged. 'Anyone can be a Murderer,' he said.

The phrase rang in Nathan's ears. He was beginning to understand why *Macbeth* was thought to be an unlucky play. Its ever-tightening spiderweb of desperation seemed to enmesh Nathan himself. Then Edge waylaid him on the way home, jumping down from his perch on top of a bin of Council road-grit.

'Hi,' said Nathan. 'What you been doing?'

'Helping out in a garage,' said Edge. 'Got something to show you.' He dug in the pocket of his bomber jacket and pulled out a bunch of keys, giving Nathan a brief glimpse of them clenched in his hand before he stuffed them away from view.

'Car keys,' said Nathan. 'How did you get them?'

'Off a bloke in the garage,' said Edge. 'They're old ones from knackered cars, but they'll open doors. Not modern stuff. Things like old Ford Cortinas.'

Nathan felt his scalp prickle. In his mind the glass spelled out its sliding message and Kate's narrowed eyes glared into his, but he didn't care. He felt bitter about Kate. He had not dared to raise the subject of her feelings about Edge, but he was sure since the conversation with Tony that he himself was only a second-best. Kate had pursued him to make Edge jealous. And when that had failed, she had tried to break up the friendship between Edge and Nathan, to leave Edge to take risks on his own. Anything to get even.

'See you tonight?' Edge asked. 'Half seven, outside Barton garage?'

Nathan nodded. 'I'll be there,' he said.

Nathan knew that Kate would be expecting him round at the flat. It had been tacitly agreed that he spent his evenings there unless he was doing something else – and of late that had been increasingly difficult. His excursions with Edge had been masked by a series of excuses about visits to fictitious relatives. Conversely, his explanation to his mother for his evening absences was that Kate helped him with his homework – and indeed, at some point in their evening's activities, they sometimes did produce enough work to fend off any particularly threatening teacher. But tonight was going to be difficult.

Nathan thought up his cover-story carefully, then rang Kate up. But before he could begin his yarn about putting up a shelf for arthritic Auntie Mabel in Beckenham, his mother came into the room and sat down with the *Guardian*.

'You're going out with Edge,' said Kate as Nathan's words petered out.

'I promised,' said Nathan. Edge would be waiting at the garage. Tonight he would find a car.

'You mustn't,' said Kate. She sounded urgent. 'We did the glass game last night, and it was still Macbeth. I wasn't going to tell you, Nat, but it's tonight. The thing that's going to happen.'

'I've got to,' said Nathan. It was so difficult to say anything with his mother in the room. 'It's about – work. He'll be careless on his own. I mean, more careless. I said I'd help.' He hoped his mother would assume he was talking about homework.

Kate's voice was close in his ear. 'I'm coming round to your house,' she said. 'And if you're not there, I'm going to ring the police.'

Nathan felt the breath go out of him like the air out of a tyre. Anyone can be a murderer. Mr Martin's words echoed grimly in his mind. Going out with Edge had been the only thing which sprang freely from his true self. And Kate Lee had murdered it.

Edge was not at school the next day. Sunk in gloom, Nathan slouched down to the hall with the others for Assembly and sat through a raggedly-sung hymn. Mr Lombard rustled his papers and then abandoned them. He leaned his knuckles on the table. Then he stood up straight, frowning, and Nathan knew something was terribly wrong.

'I have some very grave news to tell you,' began the Headmaster. 'It is the more grave because what has happened is the result of a piece of criminal behaviour, but it saddens me none the less for that reason. Last night one of our boys, Gavin Egerton, went for what is known as a joy-ride in a stolen car. He was seen by the police, who gave chase. In trying to escape, he crashed the car and was killed.'

There was a general gasp and Nathan saw Kate put her hands over her face. His head seemed weirdly light and his knees and wrists felt as if they were powerless. Mr Lombard was still talking, but Nathan didn't know what the words meant. Suddenly he knew he was going to be sick. Amid protests from those whose feet he stumbled over, he pushed his way along the row and bolted out of the hall.

★   ★   ★

Kate, white-faced in the fifth-form common room afterwards, was full of denials. 'You know it wasn't me,' she said to Nathan wretchedly. 'I was at your house. And I never *meant* it about ringing the police – you don't think I really would, do you? It had to happen, Nat. The glass said so.'

Nathan shook his head dumbly. He still felt rather ill. 'Doesn't matter,' he managed to say. Nothing mattered now.

★   ★   ★

Mr Martin was sympathetic. 'It's a hell of a shock, Nathan,' he said. 'You're going to feel very knocked-out for quite a long time. Look, if you can't cope with doing the play, we'll defer the whole thing until next term. I know Mark Bailey's your understudy, but –' He shrugged, and Nathan understood. Mark tried hard, but he'd be useless. 'It's all right,' he said. 'I'll do it. I'd rather.'

'If you're sure,' said Mr Martin.

★   ★   ★

Nathan was sure. He felt very odd, as if Edge was closer to him than he had ever been in life. After her single outburst in the common room, Kate did not come near him and Nathan knew there would be no question of ever going to see her again. The tension which had held them together had snapped like a broken cable with Edge's death. In Nathan's mind there was a strange emptiness. He remembered his lines for Macbeth and he remembered Edge's occasional grin, his ratty hair and the thumbs-up sign as he had leaned from the bus that night. Otherwise there was nothing.

★   ★   ★

The cast gathered for a lunchtime rehearsal, looking very subdued. Mr Martin spoke briefly about what had happened, then said, 'The old phrase is true. The show must go on – right?' Everyone nodded. Mr Martin turned to Tony Green and asked, 'Are you all right to take over Macduff?'

'I know the words pretty well,' said Tony. His round face was puckered with embarrassment and deprecatory willingness. Somewhere in Nathan's mind Edge grinned and said, 'So bloody anxious to please.'

'The difficult thing is going to be the fight,' said Mr Martin. 'You'll have your work cut out to learn the moves, Tony. And it's the climax of the play. Pretty vital to get it right.'

'He'll never get it right,' said Edge in Nathan's mind, and somehow there was the glass as well, sliding from letter to letter. 'Go away,' Nathan said to it. 'You've done your job now. It's all finished.' Edge grinned, and Nathan said, 'You can shut up, too. Poor old Tony's doing his best.'

Mr Martin was putting chalk marks on the floor as he had done when Nathan and Edge were working out the fight weeks ago. Taking Nathan's place himself, he walked Tony through the fight and showed him each move. 'We'll hope to use proper swords on the night,' he said, 'but it's wooden ones for now, in the interest of safety.'

Tony tried his best, but he had no natural rhythm. Swiping at Nathan with the wooden sword, he hit the corner of the grand piano and split the blade lengthwise. Nathan, too, felt himself moving like a zombie, heavy-limbed and slow. 'Right pair of cripples you two are,' Edge mocked as Tony, with a sheepish grin, pulled off the split strip of wood from his sword. Why did the glass keep sliding, Nathan thought, shaking his head to try and establish some reality. All that was over.

Kate was watching him from the side of the stage and,

although she did not matter any more, Nathan knew she understood. 'It's all right, Nat,' she said clearly. 'You're going to be fine.'

'Right,' said Mr Martin. 'Let's try it again.'

Suddenly everything was easy. Ignoring the maladroit Tony, Nathan put Edge in his place and fenced with him as they had always done. Feint – parry – lunge. It was like a ballet. Back three steps, deliberately mistime the parry, be open to Macduff's attack. Be ready to collapse over the blade slipped under the arm. Looks okay to the audience.

'Tony, *lunge!*' shouted Mr Martin.

Tony lunged. The point of the broken wooden sword was skewer-thin. And he missed the gap under the arm, striking Nathan full in the chest with his whole weight.

Nathan was fleetingly conscious of a sense of absurdity before the pain and the sound of people screaming combined to overwhelm him, and the glass at last stopped sliding.

'Hi,' said Edge casually. 'Glad you made it.'

Nathan grinned. Edge never expected anything, he thought. But then, in the last moments of his awareness, useless grief flooded through him. There was nothing to expect, ever again.

Not at Home

by

Jean Richardson

There were no lights in the bike shed and the bushes round about, which in daylight were an insignificant school-uniform green, loomed menacingly and cast fingers of shadow over the path.

Fetching her bike was the thing Alison hated most about staying late at school, though she usually had Joanne's cheerful company and the two of them together were brave enough to enjoy a few shivers. But Joanne had a sore throat, and although she had insisted on coming to school because it was English and she wanted her essay back, she had no voice for choir practice.

'But it was worth it,' she told Alison, her face flushed with pleasure and a temperature. '"A minus and a nice feeling for words."'

It would have been showing off in anyone else, but Alison knew how much being good at English mattered to Joanne. It made up for not being good at sport and a coward at vaulting and climbing a rope.

'You'd be up it fast enough if there was a fire,' Miss Barry had said unsympathetically, and several girls who were jealous of Joanne had tittered.

But Joanne didn't care. She felt she was the wrong shape to climb a rope and saw herself, in an emergency, being saved by a handsome fireman. She was always making up stories. It was she who referred to the old bike at the far end of the shed as a skeleton and suggested that the school caretaker lurked there after dark, hoping to catch a nice plump little girl for his supper.

It was nonsense, of course. Old Trayner didn't look very attractive, with decayed teeth that you couldn't help noticing when he smiled, but he was probably lonely and only wanted someone to talk to.

Nevertheless Alison was in a greater hurry than usual to find the key to her padlock. She had been late that morning and the only space had been at the far end, next to the 'skeleton'. No one knew whose bike it was nor why it had been abandoned, but the mudguards and chain had gone and the rust and cobwebs had moved in. Cobwebs . . . Spiders . . .

Alison jerked her bike free. In her hurry she had forgotten to remove her front lamp, and someone had nicked it. Blast! It was fatal to leave a lamp or a pump behind. Trayner probably had a thriving business in lamps and pumps, though most people suspected Finn's gang, who all had sticky fingers. Oh well, perhaps Dad would get her a dynamo at last.

She fumbled in her satchel for her safety belt. Books, ruler, Biros, and something that felt like crumbs or sand. No, it wasn't there. Then she remembered that it had wrapped itself round a book and she had put it in her desk. The door was probably still unlocked, but she didn't fancy crossing the dark hall and going upstairs and along the corridor to 2B. Schools were designed to be full of people; empty they were scary places, unnaturally quiet, as though everyone was dead. She'd have to do without her belt. It surely wouldn't matter just for once, though she had promised to wear it every day. It was something her mother had insisted on when she agreed to let Alison cycle to school.

She wedged her satchel in her basket and patted her saddle. Although she wouldn't have admitted it to Joanne, Alison thought of her bike as a trusty steed, and it was comforting to feel that she had an ally who would help her make a quick getaway.

She decided to risk cycling down the drive. They were

not supposed to, but there were no lights in the head's study and she doubted whether Miss Cliffe, who lived opposite the school and was fond of keeping an eye on things even when off-duty, would be glued to her window on a winter evening. More likely she'd be toasting her sturdy legs in front of the fire.

It seemed much darker without a front lamp, though its light was only small and wavering. The damp air tangled Alison's hair into frizzy curls and she shivered. They didn't have real fogs nowadays, not the kind you read about in Dickens, where people had to grope their way through the streets, but there were rags of mist and the street lamps had garish yellow haloes.

Alison sang to herself as she cycled along.

'The holly bears a berry as red as any blood,
And Mary bore sweet Jesus Christ for to do poor
    sinners good.'

They had been practising for the end-of-term concert, and her head rang with glorias and tidings of comfort and joy. It was less than a month to Christmas, and the very thought warmed her.

She reached a crossroads and now had to turn right into the main road. It was always a moment she dreaded, because the traffic raced along and she hadn't the nerve to take a quick chance.

She looked to the right, to the left, and then to the right again and stuck her arm out, though it seemed daft to signal when she wasn't very visible. She was halfway across when a car shot out impatiently from the other side of the crossroads. Startled, Alison swerved and then wobbled as her shoe slipped off the pedal and grazed the road, and at that moment a container lorry as tall as a house and as long as a train came hurtling towards her. It was going fast, and the swish of its hot breath seemed to suck her in towards the giant tyres. It happened so quickly: she felt as though she were being drawn into a black void while two red eyes, which she realised afterwards must have been the brake lights of the car, blazed fiercely before being extinguished by the mist.

And then Alison found herself alone in the road. She was trembling, and she felt off-balance and as though her body didn't quite belong to her. Her heart was still pounding as she began to push her bike along, but it was too far to walk all the way. 'It's like falling off a horse,' she told herself. 'I must get on again or I shall lose my nerve.'

If only Mum would be there when she got home, but her mother worked part-time and had a late meeting. Peter might be home, but he wasn't prepared to say what he was up to these days, at least not to a sister. Alison enjoyed getting her own tea, but having the house all to herself was a bit creepy, especially at first, when it was so still she thought someone was there and holding his breath.

She turned into the Avenue, and took the third turning on the right and then down Fernhead. The houses were semi-detached, with bay windows and stubby front gardens behind privet hedges. Mum had promised to leave the light on, but she must have forgotten for the house was in darkness.

Alison pushed open the gate with her bike. The hedge seemed taller than usual and showered her with rain-drops. It really was time Dad cut it, though he always said as an excuse that hedges didn't grow in winter. She scrabbled in her pocket for the key. Soggy tissues . . . purse . . . the button off her raincoat . . . here it was. She felt for the lock and opened the door. The light switch was halfway along the wall, which meant that she had to plunge into blackness.

In her haste she banged her knee on something hard with a sharp corner. It took her by surprise and her heart thumped as she felt for the switch and pressed it down.

She had banged her knee on a large carved wooden chest that she had never seen before. She sensed at once that the hall was different. The carpet was the same. And there was that mark on it where Peter had upset a tin of paint. The walls were the same colour, but the two watercolours her gran had done on holiday were missing and in their place was a poster advertising a railway museum.

Alison looked round in bewilderment. She was in two minds about shutting the front door, because it seemed more frightening inside than out. Was she seeing things? Was she in the right house? She looked down at the telephone standing on the mysterious wooden chest and checked. Yes, it was the right number. Of course it was. Her mother was fond of saying they needed a change, and swapping round the pictures was just the sort of thing she liked doing. And it was just like her to forget to tell them that she'd bought a chest, because her father would then point out that they didn't need a chest because they'd got enough old junk of their own already. Yes, that must be what had happened.

She shut the front door and went upstairs to her room.

Only it wasn't her room any more. It belonged to someone who could have been about her age, but this person had a scarlet chest of drawers and wardrobe with a desk unit slotted between them. They were so much what Alison herself would have liked, that for a moment she wondered whether her parents had got rid of the old wardrobe that had belonged to Gran and the rickety table she used as a desk, and bought these smart units as a giant Christmas present.

But what had they done with her things? The clothes spilling out of the wardrobe weren't hers. She didn't wear long skirts or that vivid shade of pink. And what had Mum done with her books and the old toys that she couldn't bear to throw away . . .?

She went along the landing into Peter's room. It was even untidier than usual: there were stacks of computer magazines and a workbench strewn with little tins of paint and brushes and glue and a half-finished model aeroplane. That was something Peter would never have the patience to make.

Alison was standing in the doorway of her parents' transformed bedroom when she heard the front door open.

It must be Peter, and she was about to call out and run downstairs to him when something stopped her. Everything was so different, so unexpected, that perhaps Peter might be changed in some dreadful way too.

She tiptoed across to the stairs, aware that she didn't want to be seen. She heard voices, and then someone slammed the front door.

'Danny! You've let the cat out.' It was a woman's voice.

'It wasn't my fault. He ran out before I could stop him.' The boy sounded younger than Peter.

'Well, don't blame me if he gets run over. You know how dangerous that road is. The Walkers' cat was killed last week and the traffic shoots along now it's one-way.'

'It doesn't make any difference if you let him out at the back. He's learned how to get round.' This was a girl, who went into the front room and switched on the television while the boy and the woman disappeared into the kitchen. Alison heard a tap running and then the sound of a kettle being plugged in.

She felt an intruder. They sounded like a normal family coming back to their own home, and what would they do when they found a stranger there? Would they believe that it had been her home that morning, that she and her brother and her parents had lived there for the past seven years? More likely they'd think she'd broken in and send for the police. And would *they* believe her? Alison saw herself trying to convince a disbelieving unsympathetic inspector that she had left the house that very morning and that the key that opened the front door was hers . . .

No, she must get out of the house as quickly as possible.

'It's upstairs. I'll go and get it.' The boy appeared in the hall and Alison ducked back into her bedroom. She held her breath as she heard him run up the stairs. Please let whatever he wanted be in his own room!

The door was just open, and she saw the boy go past with a jersey. There was a smell of frying, and Alison thought longingly of her own tea. She had been planning to have fish fingers and baked beans with oven-ready chips.

'In here or in there?' called the woman.

'In here. I want to watch tele.'

'Well, come and get it.'

There was a clatter of knives and forks and people went to and from the kitchen. Alison moved to the top of the stairs. The front-room door was shut and they all seemed to be in there having their tea. Please don't let them have forgotten the salt or the ketchup!

She slid down the stairs, ran to the front door and out into the night. Something jumped on her and she half-screamed before she realised that it was the cat. It was as startled as she was, and fled under the hedge.

At least her bike was still there, invisible in the shadows. She grabbed it and stumbled out into the street. There seemed to be more traffic than usual, coming towards her on both sides of the road, and she remembered the woman saying that it was a one-way street. But it hadn't been. Not that morning.

I must have made a mistake, she told herself. It's the wrong street but somehow my key fitted their front door. Was it possible? But the phone number was the right one and the sign at the end of the street, when she reached it, said unmistakably 'Fernhead Road'.

Alison was near to tears. She was cold and frightened and alone, and she longed for her mother and the safety and security of her own home. Even Peter would have been welcome. He must be due home whatever he'd been up to, and he would find everything changed as she had done.

She cycled past the little public garden that always shut early in winter. That at least looked the same. She was now approaching the high street where there was a straggling parade of shops. There was Aziz where they bought sweets and newspapers, the Chinese takeaway, a fish and chip shop and a pub called The Frog and Nightdress. There couldn't be another pub with a name like that! Home must be somewhere nearby. Perhaps if she were to go back to Fernhead Road she would find that it had all been some ghastly mistake or a bad dream.

And then Alison saw that something had changed. On Saturday she had noticed a new hoarding that had gone up on some waste ground at one end of the shops. It said that the site had been acquired by a chain of supermarkets and now, only four days later, there was the new supermarket.

Wonderingly she wheeled her bike towards it. There was even a rack of cycles outside, and as though in a dream she parked hers and went in.

It was the largest supermarket she had ever seen. Avenues of shelves stretched away into the distance and frozen cabinets half a mile long were stacked with regiments of turkeys, ducks and geese. Boxes of mince pies and Christmas puddings were stacked in a pyramid crowned by a plastic Christmas tree with winking lights, and a carol, arranged for some vast invisible orchestra, wafted through the air as though on the wings of an aerosol.

Most of the customers wheeled trolleys piled so high that they might have been shopping for expeditions to the North Pole or the Andes, while boys in holly-green aprons replenished the shelves or hurried up and down the aisles checking queries relayed to them by two-way radio. Some of them didn't look much older than Alison, and she tried to pluck up the courage to speak to a boy who was shovelling brazils into a counter of nuts. There was something familiar about him, she realised. He reminded her of Sean Maloney, who was in her class, but it couldn't be him because they weren't allowed to take jobs, even part-time. She knew there were lots of Maloneys, so he must be an older brother with the same tight coppery curls.

But what could she say? He'd think she was a nutter if she asked him how they could possibly have built, stocked and staffed a supermarket in four days!

She had just decided to ask him, as an opener, where the milk was, when she saw a familiar face further down the aisle. It was Joanne's mother, Mrs Cullen, and she was reaching for some mince pies.

It was better than the best Christmas present. Everything was going to be all right, even if it was rather puzzling. She would tell Mrs Cullen about the house and perhaps go back and have tea with Joanne while it was all sorted out.

She ran down the aisle. Mrs Cullen had her back to Alison so didn't see her coming.

'Mrs Cullen, am I glad to see you. I don't know what's happened –'

Alison got no further, because when Joanne's mother saw her, she made a funny little choking noise and crumpled up as though Alison had shot her. She fell against the display and mince pies and Christmas puddings skated along the aisles while the tree lurched forward, its lights flashing a wild signal of distress.

'She's having a fit,' said one woman. 'I think she's fainted,' said another, but neither of them made any move to help. A girl from the checkout, who had done a course in first aid, propped up Mrs Cullen and asked for a glass of water.

Mrs Cullen opened her eyes. She seemed dazed.

'I think she's only fainted,' said the checkout girl. 'Can someone get a chair?'

Sean Maloney, looking a mixture of embarrassed and inquisitive, brought one.

Mrs Cullen recognised him. 'Did you see her?' she asked faintly.

'See who?'

'That girl. The one who came up to me. She . . . she . . .' Mrs Cullen was crying.

'I didn't see any girl.' Several customers were looking at Sean as though he were somehow to blame.

'It wasn't *any* girl. You must remember her. She was in your class. She was Joanne's friend. Alison Potter.'

'Alison Potter!' Sean Maloney backed away. 'But it couldn't have been her. She was . . .' He didn't like to say it.

'Killed,' said Mrs Cullen with a shudder. 'That's right. She was run over and killed on the way home from school. The Potters lived in our road, but they moved after the accident.'

'You must have imagined it,' said Sean. 'Or seen someone who looked like her.'

He looked round at the shoppers, most of whom had moved away now that there was nothing to see but a frightened-looking woman on a chair. He remembered Alison Potter, but there was no sign of her, or of any girl who looked remotely like her.

Ghost Galleon

by

Berlie Doherty

My home is on farmland, in the flat fens of East Anglia.
They say that many years ago my fields were sea, and
that tides rose and fell over the fields that sway with
wheat and in the groves that are now tight with trees. I
discovered this when I was twelve years old and staying
for a time in this very house which now belongs to me,
but which at that time belonged to my grandfather. It
was in that same year that I discovered that my name,
Charles Oliver, is not English but Spanish: Carlos Olivarez. But the story of how I came to have this name, and
how I learnt the truth of it, is almost beyond belief.

It happened soon after I came to the house. I had asked
my grandfather if the Oliver family had always lived in
that part of the country. Grandad didn't answer me at
first; he seemed to be weighing the question up. And
then he said: 'If you're asking that, then I think it's time
I moved you up to the little bedroom at the front of the
house . . . Just for a bit.' He had that way about him, that
made him seem full of unfathomable secrets – people say
I have that way with me, too. Anyway, I didn't ask him
anything more, and he didn't tell me, but that night my
sleeping things were moved right up to the top floor of
the house into the little bedroom that my Grandad said
he had slept in when he was a boy. There was nothing
special about this room. It was smaller than the one I
was used to, and I didn't like it much. It smelt damp,
and it was dark and dusty. I had the feeling that no-one
had slept in it for years – maybe not since Grandad was

my age – sixty years back! The window looked out on to a grove of beech trees, and beyond that, miles and miles of fields, and the long, dark horizon of the east.

It was because it faced east that I woke up so early the next morning, with the first streak of dawn pushing itself like needles into my eyes. It must have been about four o'clock. I couldn't get back to sleep again, and I lay in bed looking at the way the strange light cast reflections like ripples on my wall and ceiling. I remember thinking that it must be because of the angle of the light coming up through the moving branches of the trees. And the trees sounded different, too, this side of the house. I could hear the wind sighing through them, and it was a comforting sort of sound to lie in bed and listen to, even at that unearthly hour.

*　　*　　*

It was a regular, gentle, rushing sound, with a to and fro heave to it; a rhythm. A kind of breathing; like the sea.

It *was* the sea!

I jumped out of bed and ran to the window. There was hardly any light to see by, still, only that first pale streak where the sun would soon be, but the gleam of it stretched a sort of path over something that was dark and moving, rolling, slow and steady, and wave on wave of it, with here and there ghostly flecks of white. My sense told me that it was the wind moving across the fields of wheat, but my heart thudded in my throat with excitement and fear and told me that it was the sea! Yet the trees were there, black, between me and the skyline, and all I could make out was by peering through their silhouetted branches, and all I could hear of the waves was through the creaking of their tall trunks. And suddenly I realised that one of those trunks – no, two, three – three of the trunks were moving. They came gliding behind the pattern of the trees, and were just visible over the tops, and as they passed behind a clearing my racing heart stopped, because what I could see now wasn't trees moving, with looped branches all at angles. Clear as anything, for that second when my heart stood still, I know I saw the masts and riggings of a sailing ship.

Even then I didn't realise how massive a ship it was till it came properly into view; then I could see that it had many decks, so the whole thing towered out of the water like a huge floating castle; and that it had three or four masts, each with its own cross-spars and sails. I saw it in silhouette, blacker than a shadow against the light, but so clear that all the tight ropes of its rigging traced a pattern like lace from spar to spar; like a cradle of fine web. And yet it was enormous. I'd seen pictures of ships like that. It was a ship of war of four hundred years ago.

It was a galleon.

I raced down the stairs and out of the house with my pyjama jacket flapping open and all the dogs of the farm yapping after me. I ran till I came to the very edge of the grove, and fell back with weariness against one of the trunks, sliding my back down it till I was crouched on the ground. The sun was flooding up now, pushing up into the sky as if it owned the world, glaring out across not sea, but fields, as I'd always known, and the trees round me stood still and silent with not even a breath of wind to stir them. My thudding steps had sent rabbits scudding across the grass, white tails bobbing like flashes of light. When I could breathe steadily I stood up again and looked across the flat plains. A harsh cry, like a sob, caught my attention, and I saw a great grey-white bird lift its heavy wings and drift slowly out across the line of the sun, and away out of sight.

'Heron!' I shouted after it in disappointment, and back came its strange, sad cry.

★   ★   ★

At breakfast I played safe.

'Grandad. I had a funny dream last night.'

'Did you, Charlie?' he said. 'What was it about?'

'I dreamt that the fields behind the trees were the sea.'

'Did you now?' said Grandad. 'Well, that wasn't such a funny dream. A long time ago, hundreds of years ago, most of this land *was* sea. All this farmland was reclaimed from the sea. If this house had been here then the waves would have come lapping over the doorstep. And I should think whoever lived here would have been a fisherman, instead of a farmer.'

I buttered my toast carefully. Had I known that already? I was sure I hadn't. But *had* I dreamt it?

I decided to pretend I wasn't much interested in the answer to my next question, in case it sounded silly.

'Would there have been galleons?' I asked carelessly.

'Oh yes. It's said, Charlie, that this coast was the route of the Spanish Armada, in 1588. They came right up here and over the top of Scotland.' Long after my Grandad had left the table I was still sitting there, still smoothing and smoothing a skin of butter over my cold toast, till Gran took it away from me and reminded me gently that there were farm jobs to be done, and that my help was needed.

So I kept my secret to myself. That night I couldn't wait to get back up to my little room at the top of the house. I pushed up the window and leaned out. I could see the line of familiar trees, dark and quiet in the twilight. I pulled my chair over and sat there, my chin propped on my hands, staring out as the gloom gathered the sky into its darkness till there was nothing more to see, and nothing to hear in all that sleeping farmland.

I didn't know I'd gone to sleep till I was pulled awake by what seemed to be a cry coming out of the darkness. I leaned out of the window to listen again but this time I caught that surge and sigh that I'd heard the night before – the wind in fields of wheat; or the waves of the sea, rolling. It was too dark even to see the trees. A gust of air brought in a cool dampness and, what's more, there was a tang to it, sharp and unmistakable with salt on its breath, and I knew what that was all right. It was the smell the wind brought with it when the tide was coming in.

And then, it seemed, I heard the cry again.

Again I raced down the stairs. I thudded down the track to where I knew the trees would be, even though there was no shape of them to go by. But light was beginning to come up, just a glow that was pale gold, and I knew then with a rush of fear that there *were* no trees, and that the cold sting on my cheeks was the fling of spray. I turned to look back, and saw that the big old farmhouse building was gone, and that all that was left was the low shape of a cottage or hut, no bigger than one of our barns. But there wasn't time even to think about that. Water was lapping round my bare feet. I heard a massive creaking, and could just make out the shape of an enormous bulk moving somewhere far out in front of me, with little lights swinging on it, and the bark of voices coming from it, and into the line of the day's first light came gliding first the prow, then the hull, masts and all, and riggings, and straining sails, of a galleon.

For a moment the sun burst up. I saw the silk banners streaming scarlet and silver and gold, and the white sails arched back like wings in flight, and the lettering picked out in gold: *La Garza*. Spanish. Then a cloud dulled the sunlight and all I could make out were the poop lanterns gleaming like animal eyes, and the dark shape of it gliding quiet as death over the fields of my Grandad's farm.

There was the cry again. This time I knew even before the light came up again what it was. A child was in the water, and he was shouting for help.

I was a good swimmer, so my next action was completely instinctive. I never even stopped to think about the weirdness of the situation but waded out at once into the sea of four hundred years ago, up to my knees, up to my thighs, and then I plunged myself in and swam out in the direction of the dark bobbing head.

'¡Ay! ¡Socorro!' the voice cried. I'd no idea then what the words meant, but they'll stay in my memory for the rest of my life. It's Spanish. 'Help', it means.

'¡Socorro!'

There were times when I thought I'd never reach him. I kept losing sight of the bobbing head. Gulls' cries drowned his voice. The sea seemed to want to drag me down. But at last I did reach him, and he seemed to be half-dead by then. He had almost lost consciousness. I managed to hold him up somehow with my arm hooked under his armpit while I struggled to pull off my pyjama top. I'd been told at school how to make a kind of balloon out of it, but I never thought the day would come when I'd have to, or be able to. I kept going under with him, and the sea choked every breath I took. But at last I'd done it, and with both my arms round the boy I held on to the float and paddled for shore. I'd never swum so far before. I wanted to give up the battle and just leave go of him and let myself drift away and sleep. My body touched land at last, but I wasn't yet out of the sea. We were shored on a sandbank a few yards from the beach. Waves kept pulling me back, and I hadn't the strength to pull myself any further.

And I wouldn't have made those last few yards if a woman hadn't come running out of that little thatched cottage I'd seen earlier. She screamed something to me and waded in to the sea with her long skirts billowing round her. She caught us both by our armpits and dragged us out of the water, and dumped us like big gasping fish on dry land. 'Mercy on us, lad, what's this ye've caught?' she said in the strange accent of long ago. 'Tha's fished up some sort o' monkey!'

I rolled over on to my back and lay gaping up at her till her shape swam into focus and I had the strength to pull myself into a sitting position. She knelt by the boy, marvelling at his olive skin, his black hair and lashes, his spoiled velvet clothes.

'He's Spanish!' I panted. 'Can you help him?'

'Help a Spaniard!' She spat into the sand. She folded her arms and rocked her head sideways as though she couldn't make me out, either.

'Tha's asking me to help the enemy, son!'

I crawled over to the boy and lifted his head up. He coughed, and water streamed from his mouth like vomit.

'¡Ay!' he said weakly, lying back again.

'What a poor wretch he is!' The woman knelt by him and wrapped her shawl round his shivering body.

'You're all right!' I said to him. 'Don't worry. You'll be all right now.'

He opened his eyes at last. He looked terrified.

'You're in England!' I said. 'I'm Charlie. You?'

'Leave him be!' the woman said. 'He'll not understand thy talk!'

His eyes flitted from me to the woman and back again. He shook his head.

I pointed first to myself, then to him. 'Charles Oliver. You?'

'¿Yo? Carlos Olivarez. Charl Olibber.'

'Charles Oliver. Carlos Olivarez.'

'Lo mismo.'

'The same,' I said, and we stared as though we had always known each other.

The woman had moved away from us and was standing shielding her eyes against the early rising sun and looking out to sea. 'Methinks the boy will not return to Spain,' she said. 'See how his ship flies home!' Far away on the horizon now, right into the sunlight, the galleon scudded in full sail with all her banners streaming.

The boy Carlos pulled himself up with a terrible cry of grief.

'¡La Garza! ¡La Garza!'

* * *

I turned my eyes away at last from the retreating ship. The boy was gone, and the woman with him, and the little fishing cottage she'd come running down from. I was standing on grass, in our field, with our farmhouse behind us, and the field sloped down to a grove of beech trees and beyond that, field after field stretched out to the horizon where the early sun blazed like gold and the great winged heron rose into its path with its sad and solitary cry.

* * *

In a daze I went back into the house. This time I knew I must tell Grandad everything. I waited downstairs for him, scared to go back to bed in case I fell asleep and came to think of all these strange things as a dream. But my pyjamas were wet, and my skin tasted salt, and I could still remember the weight of the drowning boy in my arms.

As soon as Grandad was awake I told him my story. He took it in his old quiet way, not surprised.

'Well, you've answered your question, Charlie,' he said. 'You asked me if our family had always lived here, and the answer is – yes. Since the time of the Spanish Armada. The first member of our family to live here was a Spaniard.'

'Carlos Olivarez,' I said.

'And now you know more than I ever knew,' Grandad went on. 'You know how he came here, and why he stayed.'

'He was a ship's boy off a Spanish galleon, and he fell overboard, and was rescued by an English boy and a fisherwoman.'

It was still too much to take in. I remembered the look on the woman's face, and the thought of how she'd pitied the enemy and taken him into her house. If she hadn't . . . if Carlos hadn't been rescued from the sea . . . he'd have died out there. And none of us would have been born. Not me, nor my Dad, nor my Grandad, nor any of the long line of boys stretching right back to the sixteenth century. The thought of it all made me dizzy.

'Grandad, did the same thing happen to you when you slept up in that room? Is that why you wanted me to sleep up there?'

He shook his head. 'I thought I heard the sea when I slept up there. It puzzled me, but I never saw it. Your Dad heard it too, and as a child it frightened him. My father told me he saw the sea, and heard the creakings of an enormous ship of some sort. And we've all heard the same cry out there at dawn. I don't think anyone ever saw the ghost galleon before you did, Charlie. And I don't suppose anyone will, now. It won't come back.'

'Why not?' I asked. In spite of all the terrible happenings of the night before I felt that I wanted to see that beautiful ship again. I felt as if I belonged to it, and that the galleon belonged to me . . .

'Why should it?' Grandad said. 'The ghost boy has been rescued. No need now for the ghost galleon to come in search of him any more. Is there?'

I knew Grandad was right. 'I think I'll go down tomorrow morning, all the same,' I said. 'Just in case it's there.'

'You'll see something, but it won't be the galleon,' Grandad said. 'You'll see what I see every morning at dawn. I'll come with you, Charlie.'

*   *   *

Well, I did go down with him the next morning, and what I saw filled me with a strange sadness, as if I w remembering it from long ago. Till the end of my the sight of it will fill me with the same grief. G and I went down together to the grove, and the startled white of the rabbits scurrying over the fields to safety. I saw the distant fields of wheat surging gold, like the sea with sunlight on it. I heard the wind sighing in the branches of the trees around me, like the breathing of waves. And when the sun was up I heard that strange, sad, half-human cry. I saw the heron lift its great heavy wings and drift out slowly towards the line of the sun, and what I saw then wasn't a bird any longer. It was Carlos Olivarez' galleon, *La Garza*: The Heron. It was arching back its sails like huge white wings and it was flying home on the winds of time to Spain. Without him.